P9-DXF-889

Also by Nancy Garden

Annie on My Mind
Prisoner of Vampires
Peace, O River
What Happened in Marston
Berlin: City Split in Two
The Loners
Vampires
Werewolves
Witches
Devils and Demons
The Kids' Code and Cipher Book
Lark in the Morning
My Sister, the Vampire
My Brother, the Werewolf
Dove and Sword
Good Moon Rising
The Year They Burned the Books

The Fours Crossing Books

Fours Crossing
Watersmeet
The Door Between

The Monster Hunters Series

Mystery of the Night Raiders
Mystery of the Midnight Menace
Mystery of the Secret Marks
Mystery of the Kidnapped Kidnapper
Mystery of the Watchful Witches

Holly's Secret

Nancy Garden

Farrar Straus Giroux

New York

Distributed in Canada by Douglas & McIntyre Ltd.
Printed in the United States of America
Designed by Abby Kagan
First edition, 2000

Library of Congress Cataloging-in-Publication Data

Garden, Nancy.
Holly's secret / Nancy Garden. — 1st ed.
p. cm.
Summary: When she starts middle school, eleven-year-old Holly decides to become sophisticated and feminine, change her name to Yvette, and hide the fact that her two moms are lesbians.
ISBN 0-374-33273-8
[1. Identity—Fiction. 2. Lesbians—Fiction. 3. Schools—Fiction. 4. Prejudices—Fiction.] I. Title.

PZ7.G165 Ho 2000
[Fic]—dc21

99-56177

For Maggie and Abby

The holly and the ivy,
When they are both full grown,
Of all the trees that are in the wood,
The holly bears the crown.

—traditional carol

Contents

Holly's Secret

The Plan

"We're here!" Mom said, turning the old green Ford onto the narrow, barely paved road. "Almost, anyway. Welcome to Woodland Road, Holly. *Our* road."

Holly looked up from the magazine she'd started reading when the drive from New York had gotten boring. "This is where we're going to live?" she asked incredulously, peering out the window at the large leafy trees—maples, birches, oaks—that marched along both sides of the road.

"Yes, it is." Mom slowed down, glanced in the rearview mirror, and then waved as a tan Subaru station wagon came up behind them. That was KJ's new car. The Lawrence-Joneses had decided they'd need to be a two-car family since they were moving from the city to the country. Mom and

KJ, her partner, would both need cars to get to their new jobs.

Today KJ and Will, Holly's younger-by-two-years brother, plus Philbert (aka Nutty Dog, the Lawrence-Joneses' golden retriever), had followed Mom and Holly in KJ's station wagon all the way from Manhattan to Harrison, in the western part of Massachusetts.

"Where are the houses?" Holly asked, looking from side to side as the Ford passed fields of waving brownish grass dotted with tired-looking lavender asters on the right and woods bordered by a tumbledown stone wall on the left. A chipmunk ran along the top of the wall and froze, its nose twitching and its front paws rubbing together near its chest, like an old man wringing his hands. Holly smiled in spite of herself. She had to admit the chipmunk was really cute.

"Ours is the first house we'll come to," Mom said. "The others are farther along. We told you it's the country, Holly, remember? Woods and fields and birds. Fresh, unpolluted air."

"Yeah, I know," Holly said, her heart sinking almost as much as it had on the awful day when she'd had to tell Kelsey, her best friend, that she was moving. Later, when they'd both calmed down and had decided to try and make the best of it, they'd imagined the country as being an orderly suburban neighborhood, like Kelsey's uncle's on Long Island, with neat lawns and cozy houses snuggled up against carefully clipped evergreen shrubbery. There'd be lots of neighbors, lots of potential friends—and lots of opportunities to put what Holly and Kelsey had dubbed "The Plan" into effect. Holly had clung to that image, even though

Mom and KJ had both said the houses in Harrison were far apart, and Holly hadn't seen any others in the photos they'd showed her and Will of their house.

Mom looked at Holly anxiously, then gave her hand a squeeze. "I know it'll seem lonely at first, honey," she said sympathetically. "But you'll make friends at school, and you can have them over whenever you want—within reason, of course. Sleepovers, parties, everything."

"Yeah," Holly said, "but how will they get here?"

"Bikes, buses, parents. People in the country do manage. Holly, look! We're really here now. Number Forty-seven Woodland Road." Mom blew the Ford's horn and KJ, right behind, blew the Subaru's. Both cars turned into a bumpy dirt driveway beside an attractive old-fashioned-looking white clapboard house. A chipped flagstone path led across an overgrown lawn and past flower beds to a wide front porch with rhododendrons on either side of wooden front steps. Three stories worth of blue-shuttered windows winked out at Holly in the late-afternoon sunshine.

Then Will, KJ, and Philbert burst out of the Subaru, the moving truck arrived, and soon everyone was scurrying around telling the movers where to put things. But Holly took her suitcase straight up to the bare room Mom had said would be hers, and looked around at the four light-blue walls. There'd be plenty of space on them for her travel posters; this room was about twice the size of her old one. And she saw she had two big windows, one looking out over a large fenced-in backyard and the other over the driveway. A hemlock tree, suitable for climbing, shaded the backyard window, and Holly was relieved to see the distant roofs of at least two other houses out the other. She'd had only a single window in New York, a little dinky one that opened onto a noisy city street. Sirens, screeching brakes, and shouts had zoomed up to her both day and night, except for a while on Sundays. But all she could hear from her Harrison window was her family and the movers talking outside in the driveway.

She wondered how far her new school was from the house. She'd been able to walk to her old one, but recently Mom or KJ or Kelsey's big brother had walked her and Kelsey to and from school. Both sets of parents said the streets of New York weren't safe anymore.

Holly looked out her new windows again. Harrison, Massachusetts, certainly looked safe. Lonely, maybe, but safe.

She'd have to get new curtains.

Or make them.

"Make them, Holly—I mean *Yvette*," Kelsey said on the phone later, after the Lawrence-Joneses had come back from driving a few miles for a quick McDonald's supper. When they got home again, Holly had stopped in the hall just off the living room and called her. "Yvette would make them—and if you're going to *be* Yvette . . ."

"Yeah, I guess she would. I wonder what color Yvette would want."

"White," Kelsey said without hesitation. "With ruffles."

"We-e-ell." Holly was doubtful. Her curtains in New York

had been navy blue burlap. Would she really have to go as far as ruffles for Yvette?

"Yvette would definitely want white ruffles. The new image, Hol—I mean Yvette; the new image."

"Holly," Mom called from the living room. "Don't be too long. KJ's got to phone her mother."

"In a minute," Holly shouted. "Kelse, I've got to go. Call me soon?"

"Okay, but remember. White ruffles. The Plan won't work if you aren't consistent."

"Okay, okay. Later."

"Bye."

"Bye." Holly hung up, still dubious about the ruffles, and went through the open archway that led into the living room. KJ was unpacking a box of books and arranging them lovingly on the huge built-in shelves on either side of the fieldstone fireplace that dominated one end of the room. In New York, there'd been so little space for books that for the last couple of years any new ones had to be stacked in piles on the floor.

Mom, her round face intent on her task, was unpacking lamps and lampshades, and Will was lying on the floor next to Philbert. Philbert thumped his tail when Holly came into the room.

KJ ran a slender hand through her short, neatly trimmed brown hair as she looked up. "Thanks, Holly. You know how Grandma Jones gets when she doesn't hear from us, and she'll want to know how the move went. I think she thinks Massachusetts is as far from upstate New York as Alaska."

Holly nodded and sat down on the floor, rubbing Philbert's belly. That was true. KJ's mother was the biggest worrier Holly had ever met, an even bigger one than Mom, and Mom was very good at worrying. Mom always said it was amazing that Grandma Jones had produced a daughter as laid-back and fun-loving as KJ.

"So," said Mom, unwrapping a newspaper-covered cut-glass lamp and depositing it carefully on an end table, "how's Kelsey?"

"Okay. She thinks I should have white ruffled curtains in my room."

Will made loud barfing noises, and KJ, grinning, winked at him as she went to the phone.

"That'll do, Will," Mom said mildly. "Do you really want white ruffled curtains, Holly? Somehow that doesn't sound like you."

Silently, Holly agreed. But she had to admit that it did sound like Yvette, and a lot more feminine than blue burlap, so she said "Yes," anyway, because of The Plan.

The Plan had to work. It just had to!

The Secret

Later, up in her room, with her furniture looking unfamiliar because almost everything that went on it except bedding was still in cardboard boxes, Holly unpacked the new leather-bound diary her favorite aunt had given her. She'd saved it for this very day—moving day, or, as Kelsey called it, "the first day of your new life."

Holly changed quickly into pajamas—and then, deciding that Yvette would probably wear a nightgown, rummaged in her suitcase till she found the only one she owned. She slipped it on, propped herself up against the pillow on her bed, and began writing.

Dear Diary,

Hi. My last diary was named Diary, too. Maybe I ought to call you something else. Samantha, maybe, or an un-name, like Bound Book. But with so many new things, I think I'd rather you be the same. I guess you're stuck with the old name, even though you're new. I hope you don't mind too much. Something's got to stay the same.

Until today I was Holly Lawrence-Jones. But soon I'm going to be Yvette Lawrence-Jones, Yvette like wonderful Aunt Yvette, who gave you to me, Diary—Yvette junior, sort of. My family doesn't know that yet, but I'll tell everyone when school starts. Yvette's going to be sophisticated and grownup-feminine enough to have white ruffled curtains, and maybe even a boyfriend. She's also going to have a NORMAL family. Kids are not going to make jokes about her and say mean things, because there won't be any reason for them to do that.

Holly paused a moment, thinking, and then went on.

In the meantime, Diary, since you're new, here are some things about myself that I'd better tell you before tomorrow. Holly things.

I'm almost 12, and I'm going into the 7th grade at Harrison Middle School, where I don't know anyone and no one knows me.

I don't have:

1. My period (my best friend, Kelsey, got hers last summer)
2. Breasts, just bumps
3. Hips
4. A boyfriend

5. Pierced ears (I'm working on getting permission for that. Yvette would CERTAINLY have pierced ears! And I'd like them, too, actually, I think.)

I do have:

1. Red curly hair that I'm going to let grow for Yvette. Kelsey says it's pretty, but I think it's a mess. Sometimes I can't even comb it!

2. A big behind that I'm probably going to have to go on a diet to get rid of.

I'm good at sports, especially soccer, which I love. I wonder if kids here play it. KJ says soccer's the up-and-coming sport, and people play it everywhere. I hope so! It would be neat to play it outdoors instead of in a gym like we had to do in my old school.

But I bet Yvette wouldn't play soccer. Kelsey thinks for The Plan I should probably learn how to dance, you know, like with boys. After all, I'm almost a teenager. Well, close, anyway. Kelsey said if I have to do a sport I should stick to bike riding, which I do when we go upstate to visit Grandma Jones and which at least I love, because I could do that with a boy, too. So I've asked for a bike for my birthday, which is coming soon. I really want one, anyway, even if Yvette might not. She'll just have to learn to like it!

I'm okay in school. Better in English and social studies than in math. I kind of like science, but social studies is my favorite because we get to learn about other places. Sometimes I pretend I'm from another country, or going to another one, and last year I did this whole big project on Kenya, in Africa, where I had photos of a Masai—

that's a tribe—village and of wild animals in game parks. Aunt Yvette gave them to me. She's a travel agent and she took them when she went there to check out hotels and stuff for her clients.

I should probably tell you about my family. Aunt Yvette is Mom's sister and she's really glamorous. I guess you have to be if you're meeting the public all the time, the way she does for her job. But even when she has a day off and she's wearing jeans, she looks gorgeous. She's also really nice. Mom says she and KJ almost named me after her, but then Mom was afraid that people would call me Ivy, which is what people called Aunt Yvette when she was a kid. Aunt Yvette hated that nickname and got teased about it. So instead I got named Holly.

I don't think Aunt Yvette will mind my using her name. In fact, I think she'll be flattered.

I hope she will be, anyway.

Then there's my little brother, William—Will—who's sometimes a brat and sometimes okay. Like me, he's adopted. He's pudgy and he has brown hair and his face is kind of smushed in, but he's not ugly or anything. He's always very sure of himself. And he can be funny, although most of the time he's just corny.

I'm not as sure of myself as Will is of himself. Yvette will be, though, I hope. Aunt Yvette is.

Mom's a lawyer—Lisa Lawrence, attorney-at-law. I guess that's why she analyzes things so much, and worries. When something happens, especially bad things, she always has to figure out why and she has to look at all sides. She says that's only fair. KJ says Mom's eyes, which are blue and kind of piercing sometimes, always cut right through to the truth. Mom's serious a lot of the time, but she's sweet, too, and she's easy to talk to. She's plump and comfortable and pretty. Sometimes I wish I looked like her (except the plump part!), but I don't.

KJ's easy to talk to, too. Her real name is Katherine Jones. Kate. She's a nurse, and she has short brown hair and a neat smile, and I know she must be a great nurse because she can make anyone feel better just by smiling at them, no matter what's wrong. She can have more fun than most grownups I know, and sometimes she can be as silly as a really little kid. Mom calls her the family clown and the family optimist.

Now comes the hard part and the reason—the biggest reason—for The Plan.

Both Will and I are adopted, like I said. Mom and KJ got us almost as soon as we were born. I never really minded or thought about it much till this past summer at camp. Even then it wasn't the adopted part that was bad.

The bad part was something else, something that had only been a problem a couple of times up until then. But at camp it mattered a whole lot. And now it's got to be a secret.

You see, Diary, like I said, Mom and KJ BOTH adopted us. So they're BOTH our moms. Our parents.

And they're gay.

The End of Holly

It wasn't that Holly didn't love her parents; she did. And everyone at her old school in New York knew Holly and Will had two moms. By the time Holly was in second grade, there were even a couple of other kids in the same school who also had two moms, and one kid who had two dads. As time went on, once in a while someone would say something dumb about having two moms or someone would call someone else a faggot or say "It's so gay" when they didn't like something. But that didn't happen very often, and when it did, whoever said it got scolded by a teacher and was told that saying things like that was just as bad as being mean about someone's race or religion. The worst time was in fourth grade when a new girl's mother said her daughter couldn't go on a sleepover at the Lawrence-Joneses' because Mom and KJ were gay. Finally Kelsey's mom had called the new girl's mother and, after a long conversation (Kelsey said it lasted more than an hour), the mother had relented.

But this past summer at camp had been really bad.

There they all were, all the new campers, standing around while their parents said goodbye and left. Mom and KJ both hugged Holly goodbye, and Holly tried not to cry, for it was her first time at camp and, even though she'd begged to go, she was a little scared. And then, just as the green Ford drove off, an older girl turned to Holly and said, "So your mom and your aunt saw you off instead of your mom and your dad? How come?"

Holly wiped her nose and without thinking, said, "No, that's not my aunt, that's my other mom."

"You mean you've got two moms?" The girl sounded aghast. "You mean they're *dykes*?"

Holly's stomach lurched, as if someone had just punched it. But she looked the girl right in the eye and said, as she had a couple of times in the past, "My moms are gay. Lesbians. They love each other and they've lived together for fourteen years."

"Oh, wow," the girl said. "I don't believe this!" She seemed about to say something else when a counselor made everyone go to their cabins. But Holly knew the girl said plenty later because the other kids looked at her strangely and for the whole two weeks she didn't make a single real friend. The other girls in her bunk giggled and whispered behind her back when their counselor wasn't there. Then a couple of them started calling her "Dykes' kid," and then even just plain "Dyke," and some of them tried to hide themselves from her when they undressed. After a few days of this, Holly desperately wanted to give up and go home, but she knew Mom and KJ had spent a lot of money to send her to camp, so she stuck with it and poured her heart out to Kelsey in letters nearly every day. She told Kelsey everything, except that by the time the two weeks were finally up, Holly had begun to wonder if maybe having two moms had made her not quite normal. Maybe I've gotten too much like them, she thought. Maybe I'm going to be gay, too. Or maybe I'm just not very likable. Too serious. Too clunky. Too fat.

Then soon after Holly came home, she and Kelsey learned that Mom's law firm was opening an office in western Massachusetts, in the Berkshires, and that the Lawrence-Joneses were going to have to move very soon, right before Labor Day and the start of the new school year. Kelsey said, through her tears, "But it's a great opportunity. You'll have a new school, and new friends, and everything. *No one has to know you have two moms.*"

Right away, through her own tears, Holly saw the sense of that.

"I could be a whole new person," she said, drying her eyes. "Really new. Be anyone I want to be."

Kelsey looked doubtful. "You're okay as you are. It's just the gay moms thing that makes people act weird."

"I'm not okay," Holly said glumly, finally admitting it. "I'm not—not very—um—feminine. I'm ugly. Clunky. Boys don't look at me. My behind's too big. My hair's a mess."

"Oh, come on! Don't be a dork. You're fine!"

But later Kelsey had given in to Holly's way of thinking,

and they'd worked out The Plan. It grew and grew until Holly became Yvette—Yvette Lawrence-Jones, which Kelsey agreed sounded glamorous and special and feminine. When Mom and KJ began sorting and packing for the move, Holly helped, along with Will. But every morning she practiced her new Yvette smile in the mirror, and every night she practiced her new Yvette handwriting, and she decided to let her curly red hair grow, in the hopes that after a while it would cascade down her back in gentle waves. Kelsey thought it would, probably.

The First Day of School

On Sunday all the Lawrence-Joneses were so busy unpacking and arranging and putting away that they went out for a late pizza supper instead of cooking in their new kitchen. On Monday, which was Labor Day, they did more unpacking and late in the afternoon put Philbert and a picnic supper in the Subaru and drove past Will's new school, and Holly's, and through Harrison Center, which was surrounded by big cushiony Berkshire Mountains. Some of the maple trees on them were already turning red, and Mom and KJ both oohed and ahhed about how spectacular the foliage would be in another few weeks. "Can't see that in Manhattan," Mom said cheerfully.

They went on to a state park, where they had their picnic supper beside a quiet lake. "More woodsy and more peaceful than Central Park," KJ remarked with a contented sigh as they packed up to go home, and Holly had to admit that she agreed.

Early the next morning, Holly woke to KJ's voice singing variations on an old Irving Berlin song based on the army's wake-up bugle call, reveille. KJ's father had been an army officer, and KJ had grown up on army bases.

You gotta get up,
You gotta get up,
You gotta get up,
In the morning . . .

Mom's answering voice floated in from the bedroom she and KJ shared:

Oh, how I hate to get up
In the morning!
Oh, how I'd much rather
Stay in bed!
But . . .

Holly, sleepily crawling out of bed, joined in at the end, as did Will, from his room next to hers:

We gotta get up,
We gotta get up,
We gotta get up
In the morning . . .

Yvette, Holly mused, pulling on the new stonewashed jeans she'd decided to wear to school the first day, along with a dark green turtleneck that set off her red hair, would probably think that's a silly, babyish way to wake up.

She looked at herself in the mirror. Would Yvette wear turtlenecks? Would kids in Harrison, Massachusetts, wear them?

They must, she thought. It's colder in Massachusetts than in New York. She shivered in the draft coming through her open windows.

My black scoop-neck top looks better, though.

Would kids in Harrison, Massachusetts, wear any of the same things school kids in New York do?

The black scoop-neck is pretty New York, she decided. Kelsey even said it was sophisticated and sexy. Maybe sophisticated and sexy isn't the right image.

Would Yvette be sexy? Is she?

Maybe I should wear a blouse instead, Holly thought; maybe that's more Yvette's style. I don't think she's actually sexy.

Maybe the blouse would be safer, too. Holly remembered Kelsey's telling her that kids in her uncle's neighborhood on Long Island weren't as sophisticated as kids in New York. So, she thought, that's probably even truer in Harrison, Massachusetts.

Holly pawed through the hastily hung-up clothes in her much-bigger-than-New-York closet and pulled out a pale green short-sleeved blouse with a round collar and black buttons. Then, caught again by the cool breeze from her open windows, she reached for her yellow sweater. As she put it on, she noticed that it was quiet outside now, except for the gentle rustling of the hemlock boughs in the breeze, but both nights so far she'd been kept awake by a raucous, rhythmic rasping noise, like a metal file scraping against a rock.

"Katydids," Mom had said knowledgeably when both Holly and Will complained.

"They're bugs," KJ had added. "You can tell how cold it is by the number of chirps per minute."

"That's crickets, love," Mom had corrected her fondly, "not katydids. Katydids say 'Katy did, Katy did, Katy didn't, Katy did.' Listen, kids. Hear it?"

Dutifully, Holly and Will had listened. And last night, in desperation, Holly had tried to distract herself from the noise by imagining what Katy did and didn't do. It must have worked, she decided now, for she had slept better than on the first night.

Would the yellow sweater be okay for Yvette, Holly wondered, studying herself in the mirror again. What about jewelry? Should she maybe wear the chunky multicolored bracelet Aunt Yvette had given her for Christmas?

Maybe not.

Too sophisticated, again. Too—too urban.

Lip gloss?

She stuffed some in her pocket. She could always put it on if the other girls were wearing it. But maybe girls in the country didn't.

She decided she definitely needed the yellow sweater no matter what. It would probably be too cold without it, at least in the early morning, and all her other sweaters were still in mothballs in the big wooden chest KJ had inherited from her father.

Holly buttoned the sweater and, nervous because of what was coming next, she ran downstairs to breakfast.

Her first breakfast as Yvette.

"By the way," Holly announced when they were all sitting comfortably at the large round table Mom and KJ had bought back in New York for their new kitchen, "I think I'm going to say my name's Yvette at school." She said it as casually as she could, but her heart was pounding so hard she was sure everyone could hear it. Suppose Mom and KJ didn't agree?

Mom and KJ looked at each other across the table, and Mom's eyebrows went up quizzically.

"How come?" she asked, sounding as if she was trying just as hard as Holly to be casual.

"Oh," said Holly, hoping Mom wasn't going to analyze it, "no reason."

Mom frowned. "There must be some reason, Holly."

"I just thought it would be fun to have a new name, is all."

"What's wrong with Holly?" asked Will, slurping his milk. "I think it's a better name than Yvette. Aunt Yvette used to be called Ivy, you know. Yuck! Ivy's a plant, not a name. Aunt Yvette hated it."

"So's holly a plant," Holly said defensively. "Jerk."

Will got up and snaked sinuously around the table to KJ. "I'm just a clinging ivy vine," he sang, draping himself around her.

"And I'm just a simple tree," KJ said, laughing and extricating herself from his arms. "Cool it, Will," she added after a glance at Holly.

Will, shrugging, sat back down.

KJ took a sip of coffee and then, looking at Mom, said, "Well, hey, why not, Lisa, huh?" She smiled at Holly. "At least you didn't choose Esmeralda or Xantippe or Calliope, or something really weird. And Yvette's a family name, after all. I bet Aunt Yvette will be flattered."

Mom was still frowning. "But, Holly," she said, "you'll have to keep your last name as is. It's in all your records."

"So I can do it?" Holly asked anxiously. "If I keep our last name?"

KJ and Mom looked at each other again.

"Sure," KJ said after a moment. "It might be kind of fun."

"Or kind of complicated." Mom still seemed troubled. "But if you really want to—well, all right, I guess." She glanced at the teapot-shaped wall clock some friends had sent them as a housewarming present. "Oh, good grief, we're going to be late. Quick—jackets—lunches—et cetera. No books yet, I guess. The principals of both your schools said we should get there early to sign a couple of forms." She herded everyone toward the door.

"No, Nutty Dog," KJ said, bending down and kissing Philbert on the top of his golden head. "You stay. I'll be back in an hour or so." KJ didn't have to report for duty at her new hospital job till later that morning.

They went first to Will's elementary school, which was only a ten-minute walk from their house. Right after Will and

Mom and KJ signed the forms, and the secretary was about to take Will to his classroom, another kid came up to him and within minutes the two of them were comparing the Yankees and the Red Sox. "He'll be fine," KJ whispered to Mom. She gave Will a quick pat on the shoulder and said, "See you later, kiddo."

Mom said, "Have a good day, honey," and they left.

Everything went smoothly at first at Holly's middle school, which was only a short distance from Will's and was much smaller and newer and cleaner than her old school in New York. But then Holly signed her name as Yvette.

"It says Holly on the form your—er—family filled out," the principal's secretary remarked dubiously.

Holly glanced at Mom and KJ, but she could see that they'd decided to let her handle it. "Um," she said, "it was—um—a mistake. I mean, well, my real name's Holly, but I—um—I like to be called Yvette instead."

The secretary looked at Mom and KJ, who nodded.

"I see," said the secretary. "Well, why don't I just put Yvette down next to Holly? Holly *is* your legal name, yes?"

"Yes," Mom said emphatically.

"I'll put down that you want to be called Yvette, then. There might be some confusion at first, but it should clear up in a day or so."

There *was* some confusion at first. Actually, it felt like more than just *some*, since it was embarrassing. When Holly walked into the seventh-grade homeroom, which smelled faintly of fresh paint, most of the other kids were already there, chatting with friends they hadn't seen all summer. Holly felt really conspicuous, since the other kids had all been together in the same school the year before. And of course everyone looked up when Holly walked in, accompanied by the secretary. By then, Mom and KJ had left.

The teacher had mousy brown hair falling in lank strings to her shoulders, and she was wearing an olive-drab suit with a frilly lace-collared blouse. She did manage to produce a thin smile when she looked at Holly over the tops of her rimless glasses. "Yes?" she said. Then she smiled more, and her blue eyes softened. "Oh! You must be"—she looked down at her roll book—"Holly Lawrence-Jones. Welcome to Harrison Middle School!" She stood up and held out her hand. Her fingernails, Holly noticed with surprise, were long and bright red.

"This is Ms. Dawson," the secretary told Holly.

"I'm Yvette," Holly corrected, pointing to the roll book. "How do you do, Ms. Dawson," she added politely.

A girl in the front row poked the girl next to her. Both of them were wearing Mickey Mouse T-shirts. Only one other girl was wearing an actual blouse, but in general, people's clothes weren't all that different from in New York. Less jewelry, though, Holly noticed, glad she hadn't worn the bracelet, though she realized she probably could wear it sometime—and only a couple of girls were wearing lip gloss.

"Oh? Yvette? I beg your pardon?" Ms. Dawson looked down at her roll book again.

"Holly wants to be called Yvette," said the secretary in a loud voice as she left. "Have a nice day, Holly—er, Yvette."

"I see," said Ms. Dawson. "Why is that, dear?"

Holly wanted the floor to open up and swallow her. "It—it's just what I'm called," she answered lamely.

Ms. Dawson nodded, although she looked confused. "Well, let me make a note of that, so I won't forget." She crossed out "Holly" in her roll book, but only with one very thin pencil line; Holly could still see her name. Then Ms. Dawson printed "Nickname—Yvette" next to it, also in pencil.

"Class," Ms. Dawson said, "this is Holly Lawrence-Jones, who likes to be called Yvette. She's just moved to Harrison, so please make her welcome. Holly—sorry, Yvette—why don't you sit there, next to Julia Worley, in the third row. Julia will look out for you on your first day, won't you, Julia?"

A slender girl whose long blond hair flopped over one of her eyes nodded laconically. She didn't look any too pleased, and Holly saw that she was one of the ones wearing lip gloss.

Reluctantly, Holly went to the third row and sat down next to her.

"Hello, Holly-Yvette," Julia said loudly, without smiling.

Just about everyone laughed, and Holly could see right away that Julia was very popular.

Ms. Dawson interrupted the laugh by passing out schedules for each student. Holly's had "Holly Lawrence-Jones" written across the top. She crossed out "Holly" with black marker and wrote "Yvette" instead in blue ink.

Then Holly went to English, where the teacher plunged right into what she called "A Quick Grammar Review" and Holly found she had to pay attention, for the other kids had

had some rules she hadn't. She had to pay attention to her new handwriting, too, each time she had to take notes.

When the bell rang for recess, Ms. Dawson made Julia stay next to Holly as they all trooped out to a large grassy yard with dirt areas for ball playing, unlike the bare concrete yard of Holly's old school. When everyone was outside, Julia started walking away, but a couple of other girls stopped her by coming up to them and staring curiously at Holly.

Here we go, thought Holly, bracing herself for really putting The Plan into motion.

"So where'd you live before here?" Julia asked with a toss of her blond hair.

Holly tried to sound sophisticated when she answered, "New York City."

"Oh, wow!" said someone standing next to Julia. She was a plump, dark-haired girl with red cheeks, whose name turned out to be Mary Badger. "We went there last Christmas. It was awesome! Did you live in an apartment?"

"Sure," Holly answered casually. "Everyone does." Before she could stop herself, she added, "We had a doorman and an elevator. The doorman wore a uniform and whistled for taxis when we went out."

Mary and Julia looked at each other, and Holly's heart sank. Why did I say that, she wondered miserably.

But Julia said, "How come your name's Lawrence-Jones? Holly-Yvette Lawrence-Jones?" She laughed in a high-pitched, sarcastic way.

"It's not Holly-Yvette," Holly said firmly. "It's just Yvette. Really, that's what everyone calls me. And Lawrence-Jones is a combination of my parents' names." She'd planned to say that, unlike the lie about the doorman and the taxis.

"Which is your mother's name and which is your father's?" asked a pretty, petite girl in a plaid flannel shirt and red jeans.

"Um—Lawrence is my mom's name and Jones is my dad's," Holly answered glibly. Her hands were sweating, so she wiped them on her jeans. "My dad does a lot of traveling," she went on quickly, again just as she'd planned—except she hadn't planned on being this nervous. "He's a businessman—computers. I don't really understand it."

"My dad travels, too," said Mary sympathetically. "He sells books, to stores, not to regular people. I wish he'd stay home, though. Don't you wish your dad would?"

"Yes," said Holly.

"Ha!" Julia exclaimed. "I wish my dad would stay away. He and Mom are always fighting. Sometimes I wish they'd get a divorce."

"No, you don't," said the petite girl.

"Linda's parents got a divorce last year," Mary explained, putting her arm around the petite girl.

"And my dad moved to Connecticut," Linda said. "He's not really far away, but my brother and I don't see him very often." She turned away and Holly could see tears in her eyes.

"Well, Holly-Yvette," Julia said magnanimously, "want to come to the mall with us after school? My mom will drive us."

"Her name's just Yvette," Mary reminded her.

"Oh, yeah," Julia said. "Sorry. Yvette. Want to come?"

"Um—sure!" Happiness rushed up inside Holly in a warm glow. So far, The Plan was working, despite her stupid bragging lie about the doorman! And she'd never been to a mall before—New York City didn't have real malls—although she'd read about them. "Sure. I'll have to ask my mom, though. Maybe I could call her?" She rummaged in her backpack for the piece of paper on which she'd written Mom's and KJ's work numbers.

"There's a pay phone in the basement," said Mary. "Come on, I'll show you."

A Complication

Mom's new secretary said Mom was in a meeting, and Holly felt nervous about calling KJ with Mary standing right there. Holly and Kelsey had decided Holly could say KJ was her aunt if she had to, but Holly knew Mom and KJ wouldn't approve and she was still hoping she could avoid using that part of The Plan.

"Maybe you could call later," Mary suggested. "That's neat!" she added enthusiastically. "Your mom's really a lawyer?"

"Right."

"Does she put people in jail and stuff?"

"No," Holly answered. "She's not that kind of lawyer."

The after-recess bell rang, and Mary pulled Holly along

beside her. "I've got math," she said, consulting her schedule. "What've you got?"

"I've got math, too."

"Hey, neat, Yvette! If we're both in the same math section, we'll probably both be in the same science one. Not the smartest but not the dumbest either. And you were in my English class—that's the smartest section—so I bet we've got all the same classes. Smart in English and not so smart in math. So what kind of lawyer is your mom?"

"She does lots of things. Mostly people's wills and estates and trusts and things like that. I don't understand it too well. I do understand . . ." She stopped herself, horrified, just as they reached the door of the math room. She'd been about to say that she understood her other mom's work better.

But Mary didn't seem to notice. A group of older boys was walking by and Holly saw that Mary was staring at one of them and looking as if she was about to faint.

Mary poked her when the boys had passed. "Isn't he gorgeous?" she said dreamily. "That blond guy, the tallest one? His name is Ralph Underdown and he's the most beautiful boy in the whole school. Maybe the whole world."

"Boys aren't beautiful, you dork," Julia said, coming up behind them and pushing past them into the classroom. "Boys are handsome."

"Whatever," Mary said, drifting into the classroom behind Julia.

Holly followed. Ralph was indeed beautiful, handsome, whatever. But the slightly shorter, dark-haired boy walking with him, wearing a jeans jacket with big silver-looking buttons was really, really cute. Not handsome, exactly, but—well, cute.

Holly managed to sneak away at lunchtime and try her mom again, but she still wasn't available. "Can I take a message?" asked the secretary.

"Well, okay," said Holly. "This is her daughter, Yvette—I mean Holly—and I just wanted to ask her if I could go to the mall after school. But since she's not there, tell her I'll call KJ."

"You'll call who?"

"KJ. Mom'll know who I mean."

"Okay, dear," said the secretary. "Have a good time."

"Thank you."

Holly hung up, dialed the hospital where KJ's new job was, and asked for Four West, which was the floor KJ had said she'd probably be assigned to.

"There's no Katherine Jones here," said the nurse who answered the phone.

Holly's heart sank. "She's new," she explained. "Today's her first day."

"Let me try to look her up, then," said the nurse. In a few minutes she came back to the phone. By then the bell had rung for classes to resume. "Sorry to keep you waiting. She's on Five East. Shall I transfer you?"

Holly knew she'd be late for her first afternoon class if she waited for that to happen, so she just said, "No thanks. I'll try later." She hung up and ran to science, where she and

Mary were made partners for the year's first big lab assignment, which was to cut up a dead frog. Then there was gym and then social studies, and then Julia said everyone should hurry because her mother was probably already outside waiting to drive them to the mall.

"Did your mom say it was okay?" asked Julia as she, Holly, Mary, and Linda walked out of the building. "See, there's my mom!" She waved at a stylishly dressed woman in a fancy-looking blue Volvo.

"No. I mean, I didn't get her. Maybe I should try again."

But Mrs. Worley, Julia's mother, blew her horn and shouted, "Come on, girls! Let's go!" so there wasn't time.

At the Mall

After a short drive on the main road beyond Harrison Center, Mrs. Worley turned onto the highway and a little later pulled the Volvo into a large parking lot. She let the girls off in front of an arched entranceway in the center of a huge long building that extended for several blocks on either side. The outside walls were mostly blank, but every so often there was a different store name or door, with people bustling in and out with shopping bags. The parking lot was full and there were several cars cruising slowly around, obviously looking for spaces. Holly was amazed; she'd never seen anything like it in New York—one whole building just for stores, with no apartments or offices above them. Just stores.

"How many stores are here?" Holly asked when all four

girls had piled out of the car and were hurrying inside through the main entrance.

Julia gave her an odd look. "Fifty—a hundred. I don't know. Haven't you ever seen a mall before?"

Holly shook her head, staring in disbelief first one way and then the other down the wide corridor that stretched out on either side of them. It was lined with brightly lit storefronts along the edges and interrupted in the middle by stands selling everything from cookies to picture frames and jewelry. People, many of them teenagers, were rushing eagerly or tiredly in and out of stores, or strolling from window display to window display. Grandmothers pushed strollers and led toddlers, old men sat on benches eating ice-cream cones, and a couple of middle-aged women in sweats walked briskly past Holly and the others, dodging a boy on a skateboard who zoomed in and out of the crowd till a police officer stopped him.

"Wow!" breathed Holly, taking it all in.

Julia laughed her sarcastic laugh, and Linda looked surprised at Holly's enthusiasm.

Mary linked her arm through Holly's. "In New York, they don't have room for malls like this one because the city's so crowded. But they have really super stores anyway, better ones than here. Fancy ones, like—like Tiffany's and—and Bloomingdale's and places like that."

Julia sniffed disdainfully. "We have Bloomingdale's. And my mother says Shreve, Crump and Low is every bit as good as Tiffany's."

"Yeah," said Linda, "but it *isn't* Tiffany's, Julia. Come on, guys, let's get going. What'll we do first?"

"Hats," said Julia.

The others groaned. "Not *first*, Julia," said Linda. "Last time we were here we had to try on so many hats we spent the whole afternoon on it," she explained to Holly. "What would you like to do, Yvette?"

"Pick a store," said Mary, "for us all to go into. Or something for us all to look at in lots of stores."

"Well . . ." Holly glanced around, walking a few steps to the right and then a few steps to the left. She didn't want to pick something the others would hate, and she didn't feel she knew them well enough to be able to guess what they'd like. She was about to say, "Hats are okay," in the hopes that Mary and Linda wouldn't be too upset or mad or anything, when she saw a sign a few stores down saying "Harper Travel." Now, that was the kind of place she knew something about! Even though she didn't know that particular travel agency, she knew her way around Aunt Yvette's and she also knew that most travel agencies were similar.

"Let's go down there," she said, pointing. "There's a travel agency."

"A travel agency?" Julia made a disapproving face. "That's no fun."

"Sure it is," Holly said bravely. "Ever been in one?"

"No," said Julia. "Why would I? I'm not going anywhere and there's nothing to look at."

"There is, too," Holly said, trying to ignore the panic welling up inside her. If Julia didn't want to go, she was pretty sure the others wouldn't either. And then they'd think she was a real dork. "My aunt works in one," she explained. "And I've helped her a few times. The cool thing is that they've got lots of pamphlets about neat places to visit. Free pamphlets."

"Free?" Linda's eyes lit up. "Hey, maybe I could find something about Chile! I'm probably going to do Chile for my social studies report this year. Each year we do a country," she explained to Holly.

"Maybe we won't any more," said Mary, just as Holly was about to say they'd done that at her old school, too. "You know, now that we're in seventh grade. But sure, let's go. It might be fun. At least," she called over her shoulder as she pulled Holly away toward the travel agency, "it isn't dumb old hats!"

Much to Holly's relief, even Julia's eyes got rounder when Holly steered them to the huge rack of pamphlets lining the wall in the travel agency's reception area. "Hey, look!" Julia picked up one that showed a male skier grinning as he jumped down a snowy trail with mountains in the distance. "Is he cute or is he cute?"

"He's cute," Linda said. She examined the picture more closely. "He even looks a little like my father."

Julia rolled her eyes.

"So's this one cute." Mary held up a pamphlet about Australia. The cover showed a man holding a koala bear.

"The guy or the bear?" asked Julia. "Mary likes animals better than people," she remarked to Holly.

"I think they're both cute," Holly said quickly, noticing Mary's hurt look.

"May I help you girls?" A tall, pleasant-looking woman came into the reception area. She smiled. "Shopping for a vacation or a boyfriend?"

"Oh, we—we're just looking." Mary put the Australia pamphlet back.

"You can keep that if you want," the woman said gently. "They're all free. Just don't clean us out of them. Are your parents planning a vacation?"

"Well," said Julia, with a thin, reserved-for-adults-looking smile, "they might be. I mean, maybe we could give them some ideas for Christmas. Or spring break."

"Bermuda's a popular spot for spring." The woman handed Julia a brochure with a pink sand beach on the cover.

"Yeah, that's pretty." Julia stuffed the pamphlet into her bag. "I'll show them that one. Thanks. We've got to go now." She poked Mary and Linda, who were standing next to her. "Come on, Yvette," she said to Holly. "Thanks again," she called to the woman as she ushered the other three outside.

"Busybody," Julia said when they were back in the mall's wide corridor. "I bet she was going to throw us out in about two minutes."

"But she didn't," said Linda. "Saved by Julia," she added dramatically.

"On to the hats," Julia said. "That's my reward."

For the next half hour or so, Holly trailed Julia, Mary, and Linda as they went from store to store trying on hats—ski hats, caps with visors, turbans, picture hats; hats decorated with flowers, ribbons, scarves, and spangles. Even though Linda had complained at first, she seemed as absorbed as Julia, as if she were trying on personalities along with the hats. She kept striking poses and making faces at herself in mirrors. Holly was bored after about ten minutes and Mary whispered that she was, too. "But we've got to go along with Julia," she told Holly, "since it's her mother who's driving."

"If someone else's mother drove, could you forget about the hats?" Holly whispered back, tipping her head to one side to study the effect of the beret Julia had tossed at her.

"I doubt it," Mary said. "Besides, no one else's mother will do it. Hey—could yours?"

"I—well, maybe. But my moms . . ." She caught herself just in time. "My mom has to be in her office or in court all day," she said. "But maybe on a weekend."

"Nothing at this store," Julia declared in a loud voice. "Time to go." She snatched the beret off Holly's head and returned it to the counter just as a worried-looking saleswoman approached. "Linda, your turn."

"Earrings," said Linda promptly—and once more Holly trailed behind the others as they went into store after store, holding earrings up to their ears. Again Linda kept posing, and Mary whispered, "She's always acting; she wants to be on Broadway someday. And Julia just wants to be gorgeous. Dumb!"

Holly agreed, but still she decided it was time to ask Mom and KJ again to let her get her ears pierced. Since they weren't pierced yet, though, she saw no point in buying a pair of braided silver hoops, as Linda did while declaiming, "I am ze geepsy preencess," or dangling red stones, as Julia did, or tiny elephants on posts, as Mary did.

"There you go, Mary," Julia said when Mary stuck the elephants into her ears. "Animals again."

"Right," Mary said cheerfully. "And since it's my turn, we're going to . . ."

". . . see the puppies!" Linda finished Mary's sentence with a flourish.

"Are there puppies here?" Holly asked, surprised. Thinking of the earrings and of asking Mom and KJ about them had made her think guiltily again of calling Mom or KJ to tell them she'd gone to the mall. But puppies sounded like fun, and Mary was already hurrying her along past the rows of store windows—and besides, Holly thought, maybe Mom's secretary will tell her why I called anyway. Her old secretary would have.

"Yeah, there's a big pet store," Mary said, walking fast. "And they have the cutest puppies sometimes, and kittens and birds . . ."

". . . and gross things like snakes and iguanas and lizards," Julia added, but she followed the others this time and Holly noticed that she cooed as much as the rest of them over the squirmy balls of fluff in the cages.

"Now," Julia said in a low voice when they emerged from the pet store, "it's Time."

"Time for what?" Holly asked.

"Time," said Julia slowly in the same low voice, "for the Main Event. The Real Reason. The Boywatchers Club is now in session. Yvette, as president, I invite you to a trial session."

Holly wanted to laugh at Julia's solemn look and professorial tone, but the others were solemn, too, and Mary looked embarrassed, so she didn't laugh.

Instead, she asked, "What's the Boywatchers Club?"

"Just what it says," Linda explained, counting off the details on her fingers. Holly noticed how graceful her hands were, like a dancer's. "We sit on one of the benches in the mall, and we watch boys go by, and we award them points from one to ten. And when we find a ten"—here she held up both hands, fingers spread—"one of us has to speak to him. We all have to agree for someone to be a ten, and we take turns being the one to speak to the tens." Linda smiled and gave a little bow, which made Holly laugh.

Still, Holly thought Mary looked as if she'd rather go on watching the puppies, and part of her felt the same. She wasn't sure she wanted to go up to a perfectly strange boy and speak to him, and she knew Mom and KJ wouldn't approve.

But she also thought that watching boys was probably something Mom and KJ had never done, since they were gay. And she wondered how much they even knew about boys. Julia, she figured, probably knew a lot, so it would probably be a good idea to go along with her.

Besides, Yvette would watch boys.

"Okay, Yvette?" Julia asked.

"Sure," Holly said.

"Follow me."

"Do you guys do this a lot?" Holly whispered to Mary as Julia and Linda led the way to an empty bench.

Mary nodded. "Just about every time we come to the mall. It's sort of fun, but sort of boring, too."

"Are there a lot of tens?"

"No. Julia's pretty picky."

"Are there any more rules?"

"Not really. We all get to discuss each guy anyway. You'll see."

Boywatching

"The trick," Julia said to Holly as the four girls settled themselves on a bench opposite a sporting goods store—"Prime Boywatching Spot," Julia called it—"is to look as if you're not doing what you're doing. So we have to pretend to be talking to each other, or looking at stuff we've bought, or doing homework . . ." She pulled a notebook and pen from her bag and started writing. Only what she wrote, Holly noticed, was "Ralph Underdown" over and over again. Sometimes she wrote it the regular way, and sometimes she wrote it like this:

DOWN
RALPH

"Oh, wow, Julia, brilliant," Linda said sarcastically, peering over Julia's shoulder. "Get it, Yvette? Ralph under down."

"Well, you didn't think of it, did you?" Julia retorted. "Hey—boy alert. To the left. Attention!"

Holly followed the others' gaze and then, like them, turned her eyes away. She'd barely had time to notice the boy coming toward them—a reasonably tall, slender figure in baggy tan pants and a loose brown cloth jacket over a red sweatshirt. He had a skateboard under his arm and an indifferent look on his smooth, well-chiseled face. His hair, which had a blue streak in it, was in a short ponytail.

"Seven," said Linda dramatically. "Oh, definitely seven!"

"Six and a half," said Mary.

"Yvette?" asked Julia. Her voice held a challenge, and Holly was sure it was a test.

"Um—I—I guess I agree with Mary."

"You can't," Julia said promptly. "You have to come up with a figure of your own."

"Since when?" said Mary.

"Yeah, since when?" Holly was surprised to see that Linda looked almost angry. "Come on, Julia, be fair."

"Since now," Julia said crossly. "Anyway, he looks kind of faggy."

Holly's stomach cramped.

"Come on, Yvette," Julia said. "How do you really rate him? On your own, I mean; never mind Mary. You can use him for practice, even though he's faggy."

By now the boy had passed them, ignoring them completely.

Thoughts careened through Holly's mind, bumping into one another. Back in New York, she'd probably have said something like "Faggy's a mean word, like nigger," but this wasn't New York, and she was sure saying it would sound prudish to the others. If she rated the boy high—and he was pretty good-looking—the others would probably laugh at her, even though they'd liked him at first. But if she rated him low, she'd be giving in to Julia's comment.

"Yvette, we're waiting," Julia said.

"F-f-four," she stammered. Then, bravely, she said, "No, six."

"Six!" Julia scoffed. "Nah. He only gets a two from me."

"Julia," said Linda dryly, "has incredibly high standards."

"Boy alert," said Mary. "Oh, wow, girls, look!" She inclined her head to the left. "Jackpot."

Holly looked with the others, and saw none other than Ralph Underdown strolling toward them, along with the smaller, dark-haired boy she'd seen with him earlier.

"He's got nerdy faggy Jacob Rence with him again," Julia whispered.

"Yeah, but so what?" said Linda, and again Holly was surprised. Sometimes Linda seemed to like Julia, and sometimes she didn't. "Besides, Julia," Linda went on, "you think every boy you don't like is nerdy or faggy. Ten for Ralph."

"Ten," said Mary.

"Yvette?" Julia asked.

"Um—ten," Holly said, but secretly she thought Ralph looked stuck-up, as if he knew perfectly well how much he was admired. The other boy—"nerdy faggy Jacob Rence"—didn't look stuck-up at all to her, nor did he look nerdy. Or faggy, either.

"Good," Julia said approvingly. "Ten it is. And that," she

whispered as the boys approached, "means that one of us has to speak to him. Yvette, you go."

"Oh, come on, Julia," Mary said, as Holly panicked. "That's not fair. It's her first time."

"That's exactly why she has to do it," said Julia, "if she's going to be in the Boywatchers Club. You do want to be in it, don't you, Yvette?"

Holly wasn't at all sure any more that she did, but she also didn't want to risk losing the only friends she'd made so far, especially Mary, who was looking at her anxiously, as if she wanted her to stay in the club. "Um—well, sure I do," she said.

"Then you've got to speak to him."

Holly giggled nervously, very conscious of the sudden butterflies in her stomach. In a way, it would be kind of fun. Besides, she knew it was exactly the kind of thing Yvette would do. "What do I say?"

"Tell him you think he's cute," Julia said with an evil grin.

"Julia!" said Linda.

"Oh, you can say anything," Mary told her, glaring at Julia. "Like—like you could ask if he's the same kid you saw in the hall at Harrison Middle School today. That might be a good start."

"Or what's the math homework," Julia suggested, still grinning.

"He's not even in our class, Julia, you snake," Linda persisted.

"That's the point," Julia said. "I dare you to say that, Yvette."

Holly looked anxiously from Julia to Linda and then to Mary.

"You've got to take the dare," Julia proclaimed imperiously, "or you can't be in the club. Well, it's her initiation," she said to the others. "Do it and we'll—we'll make you a full member."

"Oh, go ahead, Yvette," Linda said. "You'd better hurry up before he leaves, too."

The two boys were looking in the window of the sporting goods store.

"You might as well," said Mary. "He's supposed to be pretty nice, my sister says. She's in his class—eighth grade," she explained to Holly.

Feeling as if she were about to climb into the dentist's chair to get a tooth filled, Holly stood up and went tentatively over to the two boys. She tried in her mind to combine "Didn't I see you in the hall at Harrison Middle School?" with "Do you know what the math homework is?" and somehow make both questions together sound less dumb than either one of them alone. But then she realized that, dare or no dare, she'd really sound dumb if she asked about the math homework. Just as she was afraid she wouldn't be able to say anything, she noticed that the boys were looking at bikes, and she thought of the bike she wanted for her birthday.

"Um, hi," she said, nervously patting her unruly red curls and putting on a smile she hoped wouldn't look as forced as it felt.

The boys turned and looked at her solemnly. The dark one, Jacob, smiled.

"Um . . ." *You've got to stop saying "um,"* she told herself firmly. "I mean—well . . ." *Not much better, Holly,* she thought. "Don't you guys go to Harrison Middle School?"

Ralph nodded laconically, and turned back to the window as if he were bored, but Jacob smiled more broadly, and said, "Yup. I saw you in the hall today, with a bunch of other girls. You're sevens, aren't you?"

"Um . . ." *Dummy! Stop saying um!* "Yeah. If sevens means seventh grade." Desperately, Holly looked at the bike in the window. "That's a cool bike," she said, and Jacob immediately brightened.

"It sure is," he said wistfully. "It's like the best one they make."

"Dream on, Jake," Ralph said. "It's only twenty-five hundred bucks, loaded."

"A guy can dream, can't he?" Jacob turned back to Holly. "You like bikes?" he asked her.

"Oh, yes!" Holly almost forgot the three girls who were watching her intently from the bench. "I—well, I think I'm getting one for my birthday. We just moved here from New York," she explained, "and my moms—um—my *parents*—wouldn't let me have one in the city."

"Well," said Jacob, "maybe when you get one we could—could—go for a bike ride sometime. Maybe. If you wanted to." His face, Holly noticed, had suddenly turned bright red.

Ralph dropped his jaw in what looked like mock surprise, but Jacob ignored him. "I'm Jacob Rence," he said. "What's your name?"

"Hol—Yvette Lawrence-Jones," Holly said breathlessly. She felt dizzy with the realization that what was happening was that a boy was almost asking her—well, if not for a date, at least asking her out. Sort of. Sort of asking her and sort of out. Would a bike ride count as a date? As going out?

"That's a cool name," Jacob said. "Like some English names, when they put together the father's and mother's names. Or when mothers don't want to give up their maiden names." He cocked his head, regarding her quizzically. "Which?"

"Which what?" Holly asked, confused and a little wary.

"Which is the reason for your name?"

"Oh—well, um—my mom . . ."

"So she's Lawrence and your dad's Jones, right?"

Holly racked her brain to remember what she'd told the girls. "Um—yeah. Right."

Ralph gave Jacob a poke on the arm. "Come on, man," he said. "Let's go. I've got to get to my dad's store."

"Yeah, okay." Jacob gave Holly a big smile. "See you, Yvette," he said. "Let me know when you get that bike, okay?"

Holly smiled back, again feeling happiness glow inside her. "Yes, okay. Bye, Jacob." Just in time she remembered to add "Bye, Ralph," hoping Julia would hear.

When she got to the bench, Mary gave her a double thumbs-up sign, Linda patted her on the back, and Julia, with a smile that looked almost genuine, said, "Welcome to the Boywatchers Club." Much to Holly's relief, Julia didn't mention the dare. But then she added, "Even if you did spend most of the time talking to the wrong boy."

A Slip-up

Two or three more boys came by after that, and soon Holly stopped feeling nervous about the game, although she thought it was dumb and she suspected Mary did as well. Even so, after a while it began to be sort of fun. Besides, she felt more and more sure of herself as Yvette, since now the others really seemed to accept her—Linda and Mary, anyway. She wasn't so sure about Julia.

Finally, Julia glanced at her watch—a slender, expensive-looking adult one, with a narrow gold bracelet. "Game over," she announced. "Mom'll be here any minute." She gathered up her bag and her jacket and herded the others back to the mall entrance.

"Is she always this bossy?" Holly whispered to Mary, holding her back as Julia and Linda went on.

"Always. She can be mean, too. Sometimes I don't know

why we put up with her. Why I do, anyway. Self-defense? But she thinks of neat stuff to do, and she and Linda are really popular. At least they were the most popular kids last year when we were in sixth. Last year we all played soccer, but this year Julia wants us to go out for cheerleading, and Linda's agreed, so I have to, too, I guess. Julia and Linda used to be best friends, but Linda does sometimes get mad now when Julia bosses her. It's like she doesn't want to go on being—I don't know—like, Julia's twin. Neither do I, really, but it's hard to—I don't know. Go against her, I guess."

Holly nodded, thinking some of that might explain Linda's on-again, off-again attitude toward Julia. "Couldn't you play soccer and do cheerleading, too?" she asked, and then she told Mary about playing soccer herself.

Mary laughed. "*I* think we could do both," she said. "But you don't know Julia." She looked more closely at Holly. "Maybe you and I could do both, though, if the schedule works out. Julia wouldn't approve, I bet, but—well, my mom says there's strength in numbers. If you'll do it, I will, too."

"Okay," said Holly. "Except I don't know if I'd really like cheerleading." Then she thought of Yvette and said, "But I could try, I guess. Have you always been Julia's friend?" she asked as Mary opened the mall entrance door.

Mary shook her head. "Not until the end of fourth grade. I was new in third, and—well, I was kind of fat then, and got teased a lot. Julia did most of the teasing," she added grimly.

"Then why . . ."

Mary shrugged. "I was seat mates with Linda," she said. "And I really liked her. But to be friends with Linda, you had to be friends with Julia, too. That's still true. Plus I got thinner, so Julia didn't tease me so much. Look—there's Mrs. Worley." She pointed at the blue car that had just pulled up to the entrance—with, Holly saw to her horror, KJ's station wagon right behind it. Philbert's nose was sticking out the window.

Panicking, Holly turned and almost ran back inside the mall, but KJ had already rolled down her window and called out, "Holly!"

Holly pretended not to hear, but the other girls were staring at her.

"Who's that?" Linda asked.

"And how come she's calling you Holly?" Julia asked. "I thought no one really called you that, Holly-Yvette!"

"Um—well, sometimes my family calls me Holly," she said, wishing there were a big hole she could crawl into. Even a little hole would do. "Like—like when they're mad."

"Is that your mom?"

"Um—well, no." Holly took a deep breath, and realized she had to put the aunt part of The Plan into effect now after all. "That—she's my aunt."

"She sure looks mad." Julia grinned.

"I hope you're not in bad trouble," Mary said.

KJ, Holly could see, was getting out of the car and coming toward her. Julia's mother beeped her horn impatiently. Holly put on a fake smile when KJ reached them.

"Come along, Holly," KJ said evenly, in her rarely used I'm-not-going-to-lose-my-temper-but-I-would-sure-like-to voice. "Hello, girls," she said to the others. "I'm glad to see Holly's made some friends."

"Do you really call her Holly?" Julia asked in a saccharine-sweet voice that made Holly want to die.

KJ looked momentarily startled, but much to Holly's relief she recovered quickly. "I call her Holly when I'm mad at her, I guess," she said, putting her arm around Holly. "And right now I'm mad because I don't know yet why she didn't let us know she was coming here to the mall. The rest of the time, I call her Yvette, and I'm sure I will again as soon as I hear the explanation." She turned to Holly. "Introductions?" she asked calmly, smiling at the girls.

Holly's mouth was so dry that she wasn't sure she'd be able to speak above a whisper, but she managed to introduce Julia, Linda, and Mary. Then Mary said, "Nice-looking dog," so Holly, after a wary glance at KJ, introduced them to Philbert, too. Finally Julia's mother got out of her car, and KJ held out her hand to her and said, "Hi. I'm Kate Lawrence-Jones, Holly's . . ."

"Aunt," Holly interrupted quickly. She tried to ignore KJ's startled expression. "And I'm really called Yvette most of the time. It's just when Aunt—um—Kate's mad that she calls me Holly. That's my real name, but I go by Yvette most of the time."

Mrs. Worley looked confused, but she shook KJ's hand and said carefully, "I see. Nice to meet you. I guess you'll be taking—er—Yvette home, so she won't need a ride."

"That's right," KJ said. "Do we have you to thank for giving her a ride here?"

"Oh," said Mrs. Worley, "I bring the girls here every so often, depending on their schedules. I'll be glad to take Yvette, too. No problem."

"Thank you," KJ said with a thin smile. "Well, we'd better get going. Come on—Yvette." She put her arm firmly across Holly's shoulders and led her to the station wagon.

"Good luck," Mary, who had been patting Philbert, whispered as Holly climbed into the passenger seat.

"Thanks," Holly whispered back. "I think I'm going to need it."

KJ was silent as she drove out of the mall parking lot. Finally, when they were on the main road, she glanced at Holly and said, "I'm glad you've made some friends. But I think you'd better tell me, first of all, why you didn't let Mom or me know where you were going."

"I did try to let you know," Holly said, close to tears. "I really did!"

"Okay," KJ said, nodding. "Fair enough. But next time, Holly, if you can't reach us please also call the machine at home and leave a message for us saying where you're going. Do you have any idea how worried we were? If it hadn't been for Mom's secretary's finally remembering that you'd said something about the mall, we'd never have known." She reached over and squeezed Holly's hand. "Sweetie, Harrison, Massachusetts, is probably a heck of a lot safer than New York City, but that doesn't mean bad things could never happen here. Try to remember how much Mom and I love you and how devastated we'd be if anything bad happened to you."

"I'm sorry, KJ," Holly said, squeezing KJ's hand back.

"I know you are, baby. Lecture over." KJ slowed down as

she turned onto Woodland Road. "Now," she said quietly, pulling into their driveway, "why am I suddenly your aunt? Did something bad happen at school?"

"No." Holly twisted the corner of her jacket nervously. "No, not at school."

"Where, then?"

"It—it doesn't matter."

"Holly, look at me."

"It just—well, it just seemed better in a new school and all to—you know."

"Stay in the closet?"

"Well—yes." Holly could see that KJ was gripping the steering wheel so hard her knuckles were turning white. "I—I'm sorry," she whispered. "I'm really sorry. But—I just don't think kids here would understand, that's all. And I"—she heard her voice getting louder, angrier, but she couldn't stop it or stop her words—"I wish we weren't so—so different. I wish I could have a normal family, I wish . . ."

Mom came running out of the house then, looking relieved and happy to see her safely home, and suddenly Holly couldn't take it any more, couldn't take the pain on KJ's face, the tension in KJ's hands, the turmoil inside herself.

She wrenched open the car door and burst out, running right past Mom, up the front steps, and inside.

"Aunt" KJ

A while later, when Holly had stopped crying in her room and Mom's and KJ's voices from downstairs had been quiet for several minutes, there was a knock at her door.

Holly sniffed and sat up, reaching for a tissue. Then she blew her nose and, in as close to her normal voice as she could muster, called, "Come in."

Mom came in first, her plump face sad and loving and worried all at the same time, and KJ followed, looking as if she was having a hard time being the family optimist, let alone the family clown.

Mom sat on the edge of the bed and took Holly's hands. "Holly," she said, "we have to talk about this." She scanned Holly's face, her blue eyes gently but insistently probing.

Holly turned away. She wished they were angry. If they were mad at her and yelled, she could yell back.

"Holly," Mom said, "we made it very clear in your school and in Will's that KJ and I are both your parents, just as we did in New York, even before KJ and I combined our last names. We thought you understood that. Changing your first name was one thing, but lying about who we all are as a family—well," she said gently, "that's a lot more serious."

"We think we may understand why you lied, Holly," KJ said. "We each lied a lot ourselves, growing up. We were afraid of what people would think if they found out we were gay. And maybe that's why you lied, too—because of us. Is it, Holly?"

Mutely, Holly nodded, but she kept her back turned.

"Lying can be tempting," KJ said, putting her hand on Holly's shoulder for a second. "But it can be a trap, too."

"When I lied about who I really was," Mom said, "when I pretended I wasn't gay, I found I felt invisible a lot of the time. And invisible's a bad thing to be. It seems okay at first, but then it hurts. It hurts to have to hide who you really are, and it hurts to hide any really important thing about yourself, like who your parents are."

"It hurts when people tease you, too," Holly burst out, facing them again, "and it hurts when no one wants to be your friend, and when . . ." She stopped, horrified. She hadn't told Mom and KJ what had happened at camp, because she hadn't wanted to hurt them—and now both Mom and KJ were staring at her, shock and pain on their faces.

"Oh, no," KJ said softly, and Mom reached out and brushed Holly's hair back gently.

"So something did happen," Mom said quietly, glancing at KJ. "You'd better tell us, honey."

Holly did, and when she was finished, Mom whispered, "I'm so very, very sorry," and KJ hugged her and said, "Please don't ever feel you have to keep something like that inside." And then Holly told them what Julia had said at the mall about Jacob and about the boy they'd seen before him, too.

"And I didn't dare say anything," she sobbed. "I'd have said something back in New York, but I couldn't here because I knew Julia and the others wouldn't be friends with me if I did."

"Holly," said Mom firmly, almost in her serious lawyer-to-client voice. "Holly, listen. In the long run, anyone who doesn't want to be friends with you because of us probably isn't worth being friends with. I know that doesn't help much now, but it's an important thing to remember."

"Look at Kelsey," said KJ. "She knows Mom and I are gay and she's been your friend through thick and thin."

"Yes," Holly sniffed, "but Kelsey's not here."

Mom smoothed Holly's hair again. "We know, honey. And we know you need friends here . . ."

KJ knelt beside Holly's bed. "Holly," she said, "if you really, really think it's important for me to be your aunt as far as your friends are concerned, okay. But you need to be sure."

"You need to weigh the whole thing very carefully," Mom interrupted, her blue eyes intense—still worried-looking, too. "You'll have to keep up that fiction consistently; you can't ever, ever slip."

Holly nodded. "I—I know," she said. "And I know it'll be hard. It's already been hard. And I'm sorry, KJ." She leaned over and hugged her. "I love you. I don't want to make you and Mom invisible. I don't, but . . ."

KJ stood up, after hugging Holly back. "I know you don't, baby. And I'm afraid it's going to be harder for you than you think. But we both want you to make friends, and Mom and I think you have to make your own decision here." She chuckled, but it sounded a little forced. "At least," she said, "you didn't say I was the baby sitter! Whew! Thank goodness! I won't have to move out, after all!"

Holly tried to smile. "So it's okay? Really?"

Mom glanced at KJ and then shook her head. "No," she said sadly. "No, honey, it's really not okay. We can't tell you we'll like that decision. But we'll go along with it if it's the decision you make. You're the one who has to deal with the kids at school. And"—she looked at KJ again—"we'll figure something out in relation to the other parents, I guess, if the time comes when we have to."

"Maybe it won't come," KJ said softly. "Although I did kind of want both of us to join the PTA."

"So did I," Mom said. "But we can wait on that for a bit. See how it goes, what Holly decides to do."

"What about Will?" Holly asked.

"We'll tell Will what your decision is, if you decide to go on saying that KJ's your aunt." Mom paused, studying her significantly, obviously waiting for her to answer.

"I—I think I do have to decide that," Holly said miserably, sure that it was much too late to take back what she'd already told Mary and Linda and Julia. "For now, anyway," she added, hoping that would make it easier for Mom and KJ to hear.

But it didn't seem to make it easier. Mom and KJ both looked disappointed and unhappy. KJ nodded slowly, as if she was trying but was almost too stunned to really believe it.

Finally Mom said, "All right. I'll tell Will. What he does is up to him." Her voice sounded stiff and strained, but then she stood up decisively, shaking her head as if putting the conversation behind her. "Now," she said—and Holly could tell she was trying to sound cheerful—"I think it's time for us all to see about dinner."

"An event!" KJ announced grandly, as if she was trying to be cheerful, too. "Our first dinner cooked in our new house! We're having spaghetti, I'm afraid—not very elegant for a celebration, but it's Mom's special sauce, and Will's downstairs now making his special salad dressing, and I'm about to make my special salad, and . . ."

"And," said Mom, putting her arm around KJ, "I'm sure no one would mind if you made your special brownies, Holly, for dessert."

Dinner was delicious, and pretty, too, with the next-best cloth on the table and candles making a soft glow on the newly painted dining-room walls. KJ had put up some of the pictures that had been in their apartment's living room, and Mom had found that the old living-room curtains almost fit in their new dining room, so she'd hung them. "Just temporarily," she said, "till we find new ones that really fit."

A big flower arrangement Aunt Yvette had sent sat in the middle of the table; the extra tomato sauce was in the company gravy boat, and the grated cheese was in the glass bowl they usually used for olives on Thanksgiving.

"Well," Mom said when they sat down, "I'm glad we had a supper picnic instead of celebrating properly last night. It's nice to have a celebration after our first real workday. I propose a toast." She raised her wineglass, and KJ raised hers, and Holly and Will raised their milk glasses.

"To our new life in our new town," Mom said. "And"—she looked at Holly—"to the continuation of our old life as a family, one for all and all for one."

"One for all and all for one!" the other Lawrence-Joneses echoed as they'd done on special occasions for as long as Holly could remember. But she felt a pang as she said the words. Before, that motto had always worked in both directions. Now, if she went on calling KJ her aunt, wouldn't she be letting both Mom and KJ down?

"I think it's really dumb," Will said later after he and Holly had taken the dishes out of the dishwasher and made a game of finding out where Mom and KJ had decided they belonged. "Really dumb. It's no one's business, Holly, if we've got two moms or one mom or no moms. I bet lots of the kids in your school have different families, just like they did in New York. Who cares, you know?"

"This isn't like New York," Holly said. "People aren't so—so accepting here. The country's different from the city. Haven't you noticed?"

Will gave her an odd look. "I don't know why you have to make things so complicated," he said. "Someone asked me about my dad today and I said I was adopted and don't know who my dad is. And that was the end of it."

Holly felt cold. "Did you say you have two moms?"

"No. It didn't come up. But if it does, I'm not going to lie, Holly."

"But . . ."

"No. You can't make me, either." Will slammed a cupboard door and stomped out of the kitchen.

An Almost Spoiled Day

"I think we should do something fun and exciting today," said KJ the following Saturday after breakfast as she arranged the Lawrence-Joneses' collections of cartoons, drawings, cards, lists, recipes, and magnets on the refrigerator. "There!" She stepped back, viewing the display. "What do you think?"

"Magnety," said Will, popping a few grapes from the bowl on the table into his mouth. "You know, the fridge version of tacky. Get it? You can't use tacks on a fridge, so . . ."

"Oh, ha, Will," Holly said sarcastically. "Ha. Ha."

Mom gave Will a smile and a pat. "Brilliant," she said to KJ, patting her, too. "Absolutely brilliant, the fridge, I mean. Museum quality, in fact—especially your last year's valentine to me," she added, giving KJ a quick kiss after pointing to a frilly corner peeping out from behind a cartoon featuring a dog that looked like Philbert.

Will seized the wall-phone receiver. "Metropolitan Museum?" he said into it. "We are offering a genuine, decorated family refrigerator . . . Yes, at a good price . . . Ten million? No, not enough. At least twenty . . ."

"Will!" said Holly. "Someone might want to call us!"

"Sorry," Will said into the phone, which by now was making beeping noises. "My movie-star sister is expecting a call from the Coast." He hung up and sat back down again. "Has anyone seen my new baseball?" he asked.

"The one you bought just before we left?" Mom asked, handing the dirty breakfast dishes to KJ, who rinsed them and handed them to Holly, who loaded them in the dishwasher. Philbert looked on hopefully.

"Yeah."

"Try Nutty Dog's bed," Holly suggested.

Will groaned and headed for the living room.

"Hey, remember to put the vegetable garbage on the compost pile, Will," KJ called after him. "When you've found your ball . . . Oh, no," she added when Will came back, gingerly holding a wet, much-chewed baseball between his thumb and forefinger.

"Nutty Dog," he said sadly to Philbert, who was eyeing the remains of the ball eagerly, "how many times do I have to tell you this is *not* the way to make it to the Hall of Fame?"

"There's a sporting goods store in the mall," KJ said, "isn't there, Holly?"

Holly felt an odd sensation come over her, remembering first her conversation with Jacob and then the scene with KJ in the parking lot. "Yes," she said.

Mom took the battered ball from Will and dropped it into the trash. "We'll put that on today's agenda, Will. And maybe we'll get Nutty Dog some rawhide chews, too."

"How about a muzzle?" Will suggested, pulling Philbert's ears gently and then hugging him.

KJ laughed. "Yeah, maybe," she said. "Except you can still chew things, I think, with a muzzle."

"Maybe that tastes better than chewing them just with your teeth. Gives everything a nice leathery flavor, you know?" Will ducked as KJ mock-punched him.

"I was thinking," KJ said, handing the last plate to Holly, "that this might be a good day for a hike. Sunny, cool, brisk fall air. Here we are surrounded by gorgeous mountains, and a nurse on my shift told me about a great trail she and her husband were on last weekend. I just happen to have found our hiking backpacks in that carton marked 'odds and ends.' We could take a lunch, stop at the mall on the way . . ."

"Sounds good to me," Mom said. "A welcome change from the messy case I've been trying unsuccessfully to sort out all week. Holly? Will? Philbert?"

"Sure," said Holly. For almost as long as Holly could remember, the Lawrence-Joneses had spent at least one week each summer camping in the Adirondacks, hiking and exploring; Holly had always loved it, especially the hiking part.

Would Yvette?

Will bowed, which was his way these days of agreeing to

just about anything, and at the sound of his name, Philbert stopped sniffing at the trash and wagged his tail guiltily.

About two hours later, the Lawrence-Joneses were trudging up a steep, narrow trail that ran through a sun-dappled beech forest and then leveled out at the edge of a field in which they surprised two browsing deer. After they'd successfully kept Philbert from chasing the deer, they continued along the path, which soon climbed even more steeply through firs and spruces to a rocky plateau, bare except for scrub pine, blueberry and bearberry plants, and other low-growing vegetation.

"Granite," Mom said, her round face pink and shiny with exertion as she eased herself down onto a rocky slab. "And lichen."

Holly and Will flung themselves down next to her, and Philbert trotted over to one side, a bit away from the rocks, where he dug a shallow hole under the scrub pines and flopped into it, panting.

"Granted what?" Will quipped. "Granted we're all hungry," he added. "I'd sure be likin' some lunch about now."

KJ, bringing up the rear, groaned weakly. "Very punny," she said to Will.

Mom shrugged out of her pack. "I've got the fruit," she said. "Who's got the sandwiches?"

"I do." Holly opened her pack. "And KJ's got the drinks."

"Dessert," said Will, laying foil packages of cookies out on the granite slab. "Da-dum! And"—he opened a plastic bag—"biscuits, Philly. Catch!"

Philbert opened his mouth just in time.

"I hope you've got his water, too, Will," Mom said. "The poor dog looks as thirsty as I feel."

"Yup." With a flourish, Will uncapped a small plastic bottle and poured half its contents into the empty margarine tub that was Philbert's traveling water dish.

Holly passed out the sandwiches and KJ gave everyone their drinks—and after she finished her sandwich, Holly stretched luxuriously in the sun, feeling warm and cozy and content. She realized sleepily that she hadn't thought about being Yvette for hours, and that she didn't much care if Yvette would go hiking or not. Maybe I'll give Yvette up after all, she thought idly, stretching again. All the other stuff, too. Maybe it's really not too late.

As she sipped her juice, she watched Will sharing his cookies with Philbert, and Mom and KJ sitting at the edge of the granite slab, shoulders touching companionably. We're okay, she thought. All for one and one for all. Who cares what people think about us, anyway?

"What's that?" Will said, and Philbert stopped licking up cookie crumbs and looked toward the continuation of the path, where it went farther up the mountain.

"More hikers, probably." Mom sighed and moved away from KJ. "Darn! This was such a nice quiet spot."

"Maybe they'll just pass by," KJ said. But then a man, a woman, and two girls came into view, wearing shorts, heavy socks and boots, and backpacks. The smaller of the girls looked familiar—and then she shouted, "Yvette! Hi!"

"Mary!" Holly exclaimed, recognizing her. She jumped up, at first happy to see her but then alarmed, realizing that unless she told the truth to Mary right now, in front of both her own family and Mary's, she'd be pulled right back into being Yvette again. She felt panicky inside; how could she do that?

And if she didn't, would Mom and Will and KJ remember KJ was supposed to be "Aunt Kate"?

Mom and KJ and Will stood up, and everyone smiled expectantly at everyone else for a minute, but especially at Holly and Mary. Then Mary said, "Wow, Yvette—I didn't know you hiked!"

"Um, yeah," Holly said. "Yeah. We hike a lot."

"Mary . . ." said the woman softly.

"Oh. Well. Yvette, this is my mom and dad—Dad's home for a few days between sales trips. And this is my sister, Candy. Yvette's in my class," she explained to her family. She held out her hand to Philbert, who sniffed it eagerly, wagging his tail.

Mary's family looked at Holly.

"Um, hi." Holly tried to smile at them. "This—um—this is my mom—and my brother Will, and—and . . ." She felt her face turning hot.

". . . and I'm Kate Lawrence-Jones," KJ said smoothly, holding out her hand. "How nice to meet you."

Mary's father shook KJ's hand, saying, "Tom Badger. And my wife's Jennifer." He looked at Mom. "And your name . . ."

"Lisa Lawrence-Jones," Mom said. "How do you do?"

Holly winced. How could Mom and KJ have the same last name if Mom was married and "Aunt Kate" was Mom's sister?

"What a beautiful day!" KJ said heartily.

"Yes, isn't it?" Mary's mother said. Both she and Mr. Badger looked a little puzzled but too polite to ask questions.

"Won't you join us?" Mom said. "Not that this is exactly our rock, but it's a great picnic spot. But maybe you know that better than we do. We just discovered it."

"It *is* a great spot," Mary's mother said. "But we don't want to horn in on your picnic."

"We've had lunch anyway," said Mary's father. "And"—he looked at his watch—"we've got to get home so the girls can go to choir practice. Enjoy your hike," he said, herding his wife and daughters to the descending path. "You've got a great view ahead of you if you go on. It's only another ten minutes or so to the top. Come on, Mary."

Mary gave Philbert a last hug and, waving to Holly, ran after the others.

"I—I'm sorry," Holly said to her family when the Badgers had gone. "KJ—thank you. I'm sorry."

KJ put her arm across Holly's shoulders and gave her a firm hug.

But KJ's face looked strained. So did Mom's and Will's, and Holly knew something special had gone out of the day, almost spoiling it for everyone.

Too Many Aunts?

For the next few weeks, though, things went pretty smoothly. Holly found that she really liked living in the country, and Mary didn't seem to have noticed anything odd about KJ's and Mom's having the same last name. Still, after that, Holly felt she had to work harder than ever at being Yvette and at remembering she lived with her mother and her aunt. After a while, though, it began to get easier.

It turned out that soccer and cheerleading practice were at the same time, so, reluctantly, but telling herself that Yvette would do cheerleading anyway, Holly joined Julia, Linda, and Mary in signing up for tryouts. Soon they were all practicing the few simple routines the cheerleading coach taught them one afternoon. Linda was terrific at them, and Julia was good. Mary was a little clumsy, though, and Holly felt she was, too. Sure enough, Linda and Julia were the only ones in their group who made the squad, but Holly and Mary decided they didn't mind. They got A's for the report of their frog dissection, which made up for it some, and Mom and KJ were so pleased they put Holly's copy of the report on the fridge. It turned out that Mary was a very good artist and did a wonderful drawing of the frog and its insides, and Holly had gotten so adept at her new, improved Yvette handwriting that her labels were almost as wonderful as Mary's drawing.

Holly's hair got longer, and as a result, her curls began to calm down into waves just as she'd hoped. She, Mary, Linda, and Julia went to the mall a few more times, once Holly had convinced Mom and KJ that it really was safe to go, and Holly got as good at Boywatching as the rest of them. She found she liked Linda, whose dramatic posings often made her laugh. She was sorry for her, too, for she really did seem to miss her father a lot.

And, slowly, Holly began to get almost used to Julia. "Just ignore her when she's snarky," Mary told her, and Holly found that worked quite well most of the time.

Ralph and Jacob didn't show up at the mall again, but Jacob smiled at Holly a few times in the hall, and Holly got goosebumps whenever he did. She wrote about him a lot in her diary, and she put his name in her notebook, embellished with flourishes and hearts. She'd always thought that was silly when other girls did it, but she knew it was what Yvette would do—and maybe, she thought, it's not so silly after all. Besides, it did make her feel connected to him, almost as if they really were going out. She told Kelsey about

Jacob one night when she called, and she showed the notebook page to Mary, but she kept it hidden from Julia, who still made cracks about Jacob whenever she could, and looked askance at Holly whenever Holly mentioned him.

Best of all, pretty soon everyone at school seemed to accept that KJ was Holly's aunt.

Will, who'd managed to keep his replacement baseball away from Philbert, spent more and more time with his new friend, Joey, the boy he'd talked with about the Yankees and the Red Sox on the first day at his new school. Holly hardly saw him except at meals. Will and Joey joined Pop Warner, too, and soon Mom and KJ were going to football games whenever they didn't have to work.

Holly didn't ask Will what he'd told his friends about KJ.

For Halloween, which was the week before Holly's birthday, Will decided to dress up as a robot, and he and Mom and KJ spent hours making an elaborate costume out of cardboard and aluminum foil. He was going out with a whole group of boys, his friend Joey among them, and because some of the houses they were going to were pretty far apart, one of the boys' fathers was going to drive them. "Not like New York, thank goodness," Mom said, sighing as she put the finishing touches on Will's costume with him in it. "I'm glad you're finally getting a chance to *really* go trick-or-treating."

In New York, they'd had to be content with just going around in their building and in the ones next door on each side.

Julia had decided that the Boywatchers Club was too old for trick-or-treating. She wanted to have a party, but at the last minute her parents had said no. "I wish someone would have one," she grumbled at lunch the day before Halloween.

"Well, I can't," Linda said. "My mom's all bent out of shape because my brother's going to spend Halloween with my dad." She sounded sad, and Holly was sure that she wanted to be with her father then, too.

"And I can't," Mary said. "My mom's got a bad cold."

Everyone looked at Holly. "Um—well—maybe I could ask," she said. Could she?

"We've never been to your house, Yvette," Julia said.

"She hasn't been to any of ours either," Mary pointed out quickly. "And besides, it *is* awfully short notice for a party."

"Yeah," Holly said gratefully. "Maybe another time."

"Good." Linda waved a carrot stick as if it were a wand. "When whoever's giving it has more time to get ready."

"Okay," Julia said after a moment in which they all looked at her, waiting. "But anyway I think that the Boywatchers Club should start having some meetings in people's homes."

"Oh, right!" Linda laughed. "There are so many boys to watch in all our families. Yvette and I both have little brothers, Mary has an older sister, and you're an only child. Lots of opportunity there, girls."

"Planning meetings," Julia said vaguely.

"What's there to plan?" Linda said. "We sit on a bench and watch boys and give them points. Big deal."

"Yeah." Mary hesitated a moment and then added, "It's getting boring."

"What're you, a dyke?" Julia said.

Holly felt her heart speed up, but before she could think of what to say, Julia went on as if her remark hadn't mattered, or as if she'd been kidding. "No, that's just it. We've got to work out a new strategy. Yvette, I think that as the newest member, you should have the meeting at your house."

"That's not fair," Mary said. "I think we should volunteer."

"Okay," Julia answered. "Go ahead, Yvette. Volunteer."

"*I* volunteer," Mary said. "Come on, Julia, you're being mean."

"No, I'm not." Julia smiled at Holly. "We'd all like to see your house, Yvette," she said. "After all, we've seen each other's. It's not like we're asking you to give a party anymore or anything. It's just a meeting. You don't need notice for that. You don't have to prepare or anything."

"Maybe her mom doesn't like to have kids over," Linda said, glancing at Holly.

"Right," said Mary. "Well, some people's moms don't," she added lamely when Julia glared at her.

Holly couldn't stand it any longer, especially not when Mary and Linda were being so nice. "It's okay," she said. "My mom likes having kids over. I had kids over all the time when we lived in New York. Parties, too." *Careful, Holly,* a small voice inside her warned. *Don't go too far. Careful.* Aloud, she said, "When do you want to have the planning meeting?"

"Next week," Julia said promptly. "Monday afternoon. After cheerleading."

"Can't do it," Mary said. "I have a dentist appointment."

"And I have ballet class on Tuesday." Linda stretched gracefully, like a cat. "As usual."

"Wednesday's cheerleading again," Julia said. "And Thursday's usually our mall day, now that Linda's taking ballet. Friday?" she asked. "There's no game Saturday, so there's no cheerleading."

"It's okay with me," said Linda.

"Me, too," said Mary.

"I—I can't," Holly told them, thinking of her birthday, which was the next day. "We're having a sort of—um—family party that Saturday, and my moms—my *mom* is going to have to be cleaning and stuff."

"What kind of family party?" Linda asked.

"Well, actually, it's—um—my birthday."

"Your birthday!" Mary shrieked. "Why didn't you tell us?"

"I don't know. I was embarrassed, I guess."

"I bet you're going to have a party and invite all your New York friends," Julia said, looking, Holly was surprised to see, a little hurt.

"No, no," she said hastily. "Nothing like that. We're just having family. My aunt's coming from New York, that's all, and . . ."

"I thought your aunt was already here," Julia said. "She's always around, like she lives with you or something."

Holly felt sweat start to trickle down her sides and her hands felt clammy. "No. I mean, yes, she does. My—my Aunt Kate lives with us, but my other aunt, my Aunt Yvette—she lives in New York. My Aunt Kate's a nurse, not a travel agent. Aunt Yvette's the travel agent."

"Cool!" said Linda. "I bet you were named after her, right?"

"Right," Holly said gratefully, hoping the subject would stay changed.

But it didn't.

"I thought your aunt that lives with you was the travel agent," Julia said. "That's what you told us."

"No, she didn't," Mary retorted. "She just said her aunt was a travel agent. She never said which one." She turned to Holly. "Is she nice?"

"Yes. She's a great person. And she's my favorite aunt."

"How come *she* doesn't live with you, then?" asked Julia. "How come your other aunt does instead?"

"Julia," Linda said in a loud whisper, "some things are private, for Pete's sake."

Julia shrugged, but she gave Holly such a challenging stare that Holly finally said, "Well, her—her husband was killed in an accident and she was really upset, so she moved in with us."

"So she'll probably move out soon, right? Maybe when your dad comes home? Is he coming to your party?"

"No," Holly said miserably. "No, he can't. He—he's in—in India."

Linda looked impressed. "Wow! Maybe he'll send you a sari." She struck a pose that reminded Holly of pictures she'd seen of Indian dancers.

"Yeah." Holly tried again to deflect the conversation to something a little safer. "Maybe he will. Or some of those little bells."

Linda wiggled her fingers as if she had a tiny bell on each one.

"What Yvette *really* wants, girls," said Julia, standing and picking up her tray, "is a bike so she can ride with nerdy faggy Jacob. Hey, maybe we can find her a real boy for her birthday." She bent down again, her face near Holly's. "See if you can have the meeting a week from Friday, Yvette, okay? There's no game that week either. Unless you want to have a real birthday party this week and invite us."

"Birthday parties are dumb, Julia," Mary said quickly, getting up also. "We're too old for them."

"Just testing," Julia said airily, and flounced off.

Preparations

Friday afternoon when Holly got home she found Will piling empty cartons into KJ's station wagon. "It's a battleground in there," he said cheerfully, nodding toward the house. "Mom came home early from work, and KJ's been rearranging and throwing away stuff and cleaning since she got off her shift at eleven. It might be easier to move again than to have Aunt Yvette over." With a grunt, he shoved one particularly enormous carton against the pile that already threatened to burst the sides of the car. "Ready to go," he yelled in the general direction of the front door, and KJ emerged, a bright red scarf tied around her head and a huge apron covering most of her jeans and shirt.

"Thank you, Will," she called. "Hi, Holly. You guys want to come along and help me unload at the dump?"

"You don't need us," Will called back. "All you have to do is open the back of the car and everything will pop out all by itself."

KJ, who'd come down the front path by then, peered into the car. "You're right," she said. "The question is, will the car still move?"

"I doubt it very much," Will answered, opening the passenger door.

"I thought you weren't coming." KJ got in on her side.

"I want to see the explosion when you open the back. Plus I want to see the dump. Come on, Holly."

"No thanks." Holly was pretty sure Julia and the others wouldn't think going to the dump was exactly a cool thing to do. And Yvette certainly wouldn't want to go.

"Oh, come on, you'll love it," KJ told her. "It's a really fancy one, not just a big heap of stuff on the ground with a couple of backhoes shoving it around, like that place near where we camped last summer. It's got a huge building, with slots for different kinds of garbage."

"Orange peels here, coffee grounds there, meat scraps and bones to the left, uneaten veggies to the right," Will sang in loud operatic tones as he got in the car.

Holly couldn't resist joining in, even though Yvette wouldn't. "Green things from the back of the fridge," she sang, hitting a high note on the word "fridge."

"Unidentified molding objects," Will sang, *basso profundo.*

"Odd things in jars," KJ contributed, stepping up the tempo. "Tired meat and worn-out magazines, newspapers . . ."

"Old tires," Holly added, on a single note.

"Bones." Will snapped his fingers. "Chicken bone connected to the ham bone, ham bone connected to the pork bone, pork bone connected to the turkey bone . . ."

"All de bones down in de dump," Holly chimed in, slowly, her voice as low as she could make it, providing rhythmic percussion. KJ joined in, and soon they were both singing, "De dump, de dump, de dump, dump dump . . ."

"Dump, glorious dump!" Will finished an octave higher, with a flourish.

"Not quite glorious, maybe," KJ said, laughing. "But close. Separate compartments for cans and for bottles of different colors and for newspapers—that kind of thing." She reached out of the car window for Holly's hand. "It's nice to have you back, Holly, if only for a moment."

"Huh?" asked Holly.

"Think about it," KJ called as she started the car and drove off.

Puzzled, Holly watched them go. Then, trying to ignore what KJ might have meant, she went into the house, where she found Mom on her hands and knees, scrubbing the kitchen floor.

"I bet Martha Stewart would never get down on her hands and knees," Mom said breathlessly, looking up. Holly knew Martha Stewart was a woman who was famous for being a glamorous homemaker; KJ joked about her a lot whenever Mom started a flurry of housecleaning. "And neither would Aunt Yvette." Mom reached up to the counter. "Have a cookie—no, don't walk on that part." She shoved a plate of cookies toward Holly.

"Aunt Yvette," said Holly, taking a cookie, "doesn't have time for housecleaning."

"Your Aunt Yvette's a law unto herself." Sighing, Mom pulled herself up and flopped onto one of the kitchen chairs. "But I must admit that today cleaning's a welcome change from that messy case I'm still working on. Is your room in any kind of shape? I seem to remember a couple of piles of things."

"Books," Holly said around a mouthful of cookie. "I haven't really figured out how to arrange them yet."

"Well," Mom said, munching a cookie herself, "now's the time. How about alphabetical by author? Aunt Yvette's going to want to see the new house—every bit of it. Off you go! And then please take Philbert out and don't let him get into anything! Mud, for example."

It took the rest of the afternoon and well into the evening to finish the last bits of sorting and arranging, not to mention cleaning and polishing. But when it was done, the house literally sparkled and everything in it finally looked as if it belonged.

"Too bad the President and the First Lady aren't coming instead of just Aunt Yvette," Will remarked when they all headed upstairs to bed.

"That's next week," KJ said.

"Actually," Holly said, thinking this was as good a time as any, "next week can I have some friends over?"

Mom smiled broadly and so did KJ. "Of course!" they both said at once.

"Any time," KJ added.

"Cool, Holly." Will paused at his bedroom door. "Strike while the iron's hot. But I think I'll wait till the house is a mess again before I invite Joey over. I went to his house and it looks as if no one's cleaned it in decades. You could trip over the dust balls and piled-up newspapers. I wouldn't want him to feel out of place."

"You probably just got there on a bad day." Mom kissed Will and then Holly good night.

"Remember the dust under the sofa in New York when we moved out," KJ said, also kissing them both. "You could have made a blanket out of it."

"I thought it *was* a blanket," Will said, and fled into his room when KJ lunged at him playfully.

The next morning—her birthday—Holly woke to sun streaming in through her window. She lay still for a few minutes, casting a critical eye over her neat, clean room—Yvette's new room—the room that would be inspected by Julia, Linda, and Mary when they came over. The white bureau and bed and nightstand were fine, and so were the filmy white curtains (without real ruffles, though, since she'd made them herself). But she was sure Yvette would have a dressing table like Aunt Yvette's—a low, kidney-shaped table with a mirror and a frilly skirt, and a backless upholstered stool to sit on while doing one's hair. That would really impress Julia. Aunt Yvette's dressing table had silver-backed brushes and combs on it, and lots of perfume bottles, along with jars of face cream, bottles of lotion and foundation and moisturizer, and trays of eyebrow pencils, lipsticks, eye shadow, mascara—stuff she knew Mom and KJ would never let her wear now, but maybe in a few years . . .

"Happy birthday, birthday girl," came Mom's voice outside her door. "Special delivery!"

Holly jumped out of bed and opened her door to see Mom standing there with a huge bouquet of flowers in her hands, and Philbert standing next to her, tail wagging, with an envelope in his mouth. "This is just a preview," Mom said, holding out the bouquet and kissing her.

Holly buried her nose in the flowers—lilies, baby's breath, and two perfect pink roses—and her eyes filled with sudden tears. "They're beautiful," she said. "Thank you."

"You'd better open the card," KJ said, coming up behind Mom, "before Nutty Dog eats it. It's handmade," she added.

Holly reached for the card, but Philbert, tail still wagging, backed up as if wanting to play keep-away, which was one of his favorite games. "Give, Philly," Holly said. "Come on, Philbert, *give*!"

After a few awkward prances, Philbert poked his mouth at her, letting Holly take the somewhat damp envelope from him and open it.

On the front of the card was pasted a photo of Holly when she was a baby, standing up in her playpen with a big smile on her face, brandishing a rattle. Above it was written "Year by Year . . ."

Inside was a photo of Holly taken last year, standing in her old room in front of her travel poster of the Eiffel Tower. Above that was written: "Our Holly Just Gets More Wonderful Year by Year!" Below the picture, it said, "Happy Birthday, with love from Mom, KJ, Will, and Philbert."

And opposite the picture, in fancy calligraphy, was a poem:

The holly and the ivy,
When they are both full grown,
Of all the trees that are in the wood,
The holly bears the crown.

Puzzled and a little uncomfortable, Holly looked at Mom and KJ. "Um—thank you," she said. "That's a pretty poem."

KJ winked at Mom and gave Holly a big hug. "You're welcome, sweetie."

"Breakfast," Mom announced, winking back at KJ. "Bacon and pancakes, right?"

"Right," Holly answered; that was her favorite breakfast, and she was suddenly ravenous—but she was still puzzled about the poem and the winks. Why did the poem have her name in it? Was the ivy part important? And why did it say "full grown" when she'd only just turned twelve? What did the crown part mean?

But then Will came bursting out of his room, shouting "Time for the birthday spanks!" and chased her down the stairs.

Happy Birthday

Not long after breakfast, the phone rang, and it was Kelsey, singing "Happy Birthday" and then saying, "I miss you. Are you having a party? Remember last year, when Ellen Hithner fell over the rug and spilled Coke on everything?"

Holly giggled. "Yeah, and Angie Delaney was late because her mother took the wrong subway and ended up in Morningside Heights . . ."

"And Will ate too much ice cream . . ."

"Oh, gross, Kelsey! I don't want to remember that part!"

"But it was still a neat party."

"Yeah. It was."

"So this year"—Kelsey's voice sounded falsely cheerful—"I bet you'll have that Boywatchers group you wrote me about. Unless—that might be hard, with The Plan."

"Well, I'm not having them, anyway," Holly said. "Just family." She paused. "But the Boywatchers are coming here next week for a meeting."

"Uh-oh," Kelsey said. "The Plan! You'd better be careful!"

"I know," Holly said—and for the next twenty minutes or so, till Kelsey's mother made her get off the phone, they worked out how Holly could make sure nothing would happen at the meeting that could give her secret away.

Holly spent the rest of the day reading, playing outside with Philbert, and trying not to mind that although Mary and Linda had sent her cards, Julia hadn't. "She probably forgot," Mary said when Holly finally called her. "She never remembers birthdays."

By the time Aunt Yvette arrived for the family celebration, the chicken was in the oven, and the dining room—which Holly hadn't been allowed to see—was decorated. Holly herself had brushed her flyaway hair and put on a pale blue dress she almost liked (she was sure Yvette would love it), and Mom and KJ were wearing dresses, too. Even Will was dressed up, in a sports jacket, good pants, and a natty bow tie.

Aunt Yvette swept into the house, wearing a long, full rose-colored skirt with large black flowers on it, a black peasant blouse with wide sleeves, and huge gold hoops in her ears. Her shiny black hair was swept back in an exuberant new style that made her look as if she'd been running in the wind, but carefully. "Holly, my love!" she exclaimed, putting down her overnight bag and kissing her. "You look absolutely gorgeous! Happy birthday, angel." She thrust two flat packages, one larger than the other, at KJ. "Here's more loot for the birthday girl," she said, kissing KJ and then kissing Mom.

"Thanks," KJ said. "I'll put them with the rest of it." In the Lawrence-Jones family, birthday presents were carried ceremoniously into the dining room after the main part of dinner, with the cake.

"Come on in, Yvette," Mom said. "There's time for the grand tour before we eat."

For the next twenty minutes or so, Mom, KJ, Will, Holly, and Philbert led Aunt Yvette through the house, and Aunt Yvette exclaimed enthusiastically about each room. "It's a darling house," she said when they were all back in the living room, sitting down, the adults with wine and Holly and Will with Cokes. "Just darling. And your yard—mmm!" Aunt Yvette put her hand to her pursed lips and then pulled it away again, making a smacking kissing sound. "It's exactly what I'd have if I could only get out of the city."

Mom smiled secretly at Holly—for both of them knew Aunt Yvette would never, never leave the excitement of New York.

"Holly," Aunt Yvette went on, "your room is wonderful—so much bigger than your old one. Bright and cheerful, with those splendid windows. And I see you've got your travel posters up."

"I think I might get a dressing table," Holly said experimentally, with a sidelong glance at Mom and KJ. "One like yours, with a skirt."

"Oh?" Aunt Yvette raised her eyebrows. "Already? That doesn't sound quite like you!"

"Holly's not like Holly any more," Will said.

Mom and KJ got up as the oven timer dinged. "She's calling herself Yvette at school," Mom tossed over her shoulder as she and KJ headed for the kitchen. "Will, please let Philbert out; he's at the door."

"Lambie, I'm flattered," Aunt Yvette said when they all were gone. But her eyebrows had gone up even higher and she gave Holly a long appraising look. "New place, new personality?" she asked.

"Sort of," Holly said uncomfortably.

"Mmmm." Aunt Yvette seemed to think that over. "Well," she said finally, "twelve's a pretty special landmark age, almost a teenager, and that's a big change. And of course one does grow up. Still, I kind of liked the old Holly. Don't change too much, angel." She leaned toward Holly. "Don't ever lose who you really are."

"Dinner's ready!" KJ called from the kitchen, saving Holly from having to answer.

Dinner was perfect—all Holly's favorite dishes—and afterward, as she sat alone in the dining room, waiting for the others to come marching in with her presents, she felt almost as excited as she had when she'd been a lot younger. Yvette, of course, wouldn't show that—probably wouldn't even feel it—but Holly couldn't help it, especially when she thought of the bike she hoped she was getting, and of riding it with Jacob.

Then the strains of "Happy Birthday to You!" resounded from the kitchen and the procession arrived: Will in the lead with the cake, its twelve candles, and one to grow on, blazing, then Aunt Yvette with a stack of packages, and finally Mom and KJ, solemnly unwinding what looked like a ball of yarn.

No bike.

Blinking back tears, Holly smiled as politely as she could and managed to say, "What a neat cake!" But her stomach had twisted itself into disappointed knots and a lump rose in her throat.

"First, madame," said Mom, handing her the ball of yarn, "may we present you with this—er—guideline?"

"You must follow this line, oh, birthday girl," KJ intoned in a deep, solemn voice, "before you do anything else . . ."

"Except blow out the candles," Will said, his eyes on the cake, "unless you want to celebrate being twelve by burning the house down."

Hastily, Holly puffed at the candles.

"Don't forget to make a wish," Aunt Yvette said when the candles were all out, and everyone laughed.

"Now, madame," KJ said, "if you please, follow the line. Follow the line," she sang as Holly got up, "follow the line, follow the line, follow . . ."

"I think she's got it, KJ," Will said in a loud whisper.

Everyone followed Holly as she wound the yarn back onto its ball. It led her into the kitchen, through it to the back door, then out the back door—could it be? could it really be?—and across the yard into the garage.

And there, with the end of the yarn tied to it, was a brand-new, sparkling silver-and-blue, ten-speed bike!

A Bike Ride

On Monday, Holly rode her bike to school, wearing a new striped turtleneck Will had given her and a jeans jacket Aunt Yvette had given her. (The other flat present from Aunt Yvette was an atlas with lots of color photographs and detailed un-textbooky descriptions of all the world's countries.) She'd spent Sunday riding her bike up and down bumpy Woodland Road, practicing with the various gears—the bike she'd ridden at Grandma Jones's had only three—and she'd messed them up only twice. It had felt good being outdoors in the crisp autumn day with KJ, Mom, and Aunt Yvette, who'd spent the night, cheering her on from the front yard. Holly reveled in the speed as she pedaled up and down with the wind making her hair stream back and her leg muscles stretching and contracting rhythmically.

Would Yvette like doing that? For a while, Holly almost didn't care. And she found herself thinking longingly of soccer again. Because of cheerleading tryouts, she and Mary hadn't signed up for it, and by the time they found out they hadn't made the cheerleading squad, it was too late to sign up for soccer.

When Monday came, and her aunt had gone back to New York, Holly almost didn't want to slip back into being Yvette again—but at least Yvette would certainly want to go bike riding with Jacob Rence!

Mary was just arriving at school when Holly rode up to the bike rack, put her front wheel carefully in a slot, and secured it with the fancy combination lock that had come with the bike.

"Hey, Yvette!" Mary called, running over to her. "You got it. Wow—it's beautiful!"

"Yeah," Holly said. "It's pretty neat. I was scared I wouldn't get it, too." She told Mary about the ball of yarn.

Mary laughed. "Your family is so cool," she said almost enviously. "I don't think anyone in my family would think of doing something like that."

"One Christmas," Holly said without thinking, "Mom gave KJ a bracelet she wanted, only she wrapped it in a whole bunch of boxes, starting with a little one and then ending up with a huge one. You know, like those Russian dolls."

Mary was frowning. "Who's KJ?" she asked—and Holly's stomach tied itself into knots again. "I didn't know you had a sister."

"No, no, I don't. That's—um—my aunt. The one you met. Aunt Kate. We—um—we call her KJ sometimes."

"How come?"

"Well, her name was Kate Jones, and . . ."

Mary looked puzzled. "Didn't she say Lawrence-Jones? On the mountain? You know, I kind of wondered . . ."

"Did she?" Holly said vaguely. "Well—um—yes. She—um—she goes by that, too. Sometimes. Um—professionally. You know, for nursing."

Mary frowned, as if trying to puzzle it out. "So she must be your dad's sister? You said Jones is your dad's name, and Lawrence is your mom's. Didn't you?"

Holly bent over and pretended to tie her shoelace. Had she said that? She couldn't remember, no matter how frantically she tried.

"Right," she said, straightening up as an idea finally occurred to her. "Well—um—see, Aunt Kate—KJ—is really my mom's sister, but she married my dad's brother, so she—um—she sometimes uses both names, too, like we do. And it—it's better professionally, because—because there are lots of other people named Jones."

Mary gave her a strange look. All she said was "Oh," but Holly was sure Mary didn't believe her and was too nice to challenge her any more.

"Well, it's a beautiful bike anyway," Mary said. Then she grinned and nudged Holly's side with her arm. "I bet you-know-who will love it!"

Jacob did love it, at least that was what he said at lunchtime when he came over to the table where Holly was eating lunch with Mary, Linda, and Julia. Not only that . . .

"Want to go for a ride after school?" he asked, giving Holly a broad smile.

Julia rolled her eyes, but Mary and Linda smiled back at him as Holly, trying to ignore the fluttering of her heart, said, "Sure!"

"I'll meet you by the bike rack, okay?"

"Okay! Um—thanks!"

"You don't say thanks when a boy asks you out, Yvette," Linda whispered as Jacob left.

"Sure you do," Mary said.

"Oh, who cares?" Julia stood and picked up her tray. "Nerdy faggy Jake might be okay to start with, I guess. But he doesn't count as a real boy. Careful, Yvette, or you'll end up being a fag hag."

"What's a fag hag?" Mary asked when Julia had left.

Linda shrugged, and Holly pretended she didn't know either, but she did. A fag hag was a girl who hung around with gay boys instead of straight ones.

After school, when she wasn't able to reach Mom or KJ, Holly remembered to leave a message on the family phone machine before she went out to meet Jacob. He was waiting by the bike rack just as he'd said he would be. His brown hair was shining clean and his eyes had a twinkly, soft look that made Holly feel mushy inside.

"It really is a neat bike," he said, studying it admiringly. "Much better than my beat-up old thing."

His bike did seem somewhat the worse for wear.

"Your bike looks—looks comfortable, though," Holly said.

"It's that, all right. This seat and I have been glued together for so long that no one else is comfortable sitting on it." He looked at her with the broad smile again. "Where would you like to go?"

"I—um—I don't know. You pick. I haven't been in Harrison long enough to know much of any place."

"You say 'um' a lot, don't you?" Jacob remarked as he swung himself up onto his bike. "It's okay," he added quickly as Holly felt herself blush. "I like it. Some girls seem so sure of everything they make me feel really dumb." Before she'd figured out how to answer him, he went on. "Let's go down to the Franklin land. It's got bike paths, so it's easy riding, and it's pretty. Sometimes you see deer there. I bet you don't have deer in New York."

"No." Holly had managed to get on her bike almost as gracefully as Yvette would and was now riding along beside Jacob, trying to look ladylike. "We don't."

"But you've got lots of other cool things," Jacob called over his shoulder, shooting out ahead of her as they reached the main road. "Single file here, okay? You've got museums and theaters and thousands of stores and Yankee Stadium and Shea Stadium and Madison Square Garden and stuff like that. I've never been to New York."

"New York's okay," Holly shouted above the roar of a truck that was coming up behind them. She gripped the handlebars hard, but then remembered it was safer to keep your hands relaxed. She eased up on her grip and that really did help her stay steady as the truck passed. "But I like Harrison, too," she called to Jacob.

"There's not much to do in Harrison—right turn here." He twisted around, facing her for a moment. "Except go bike riding, of course."

Holly followed Jacob along several side streets until they finally came to a huge woodsy park-like place, where there were hard-packed dirt paths, wide enough so they could ride side by side again. Jacob explained that it wasn't really a park but instead was what was called "conservation land," land the town of Harrison owned and that no one could build on, so it would stay wild forever. A rich man named Alex Franklin had left it to the town in his will.

For the next hour, they rode together, while Jacob pointed out the sights—a meadow where the deer often browsed, a pond where there were ducks and geese, a huge rock. "My dog likes to stand on it and bark," he said as they pedaled by. "Not *at* anything. He just likes to bark, like a little kid playing king of the castle."

"I've got a dog, too," Holly told him, and for a while they talked about dogs, and decided that Philbert and Clancy, Jacob's dog, should meet sometime.

"Dad and I bring Clancy here on Saturdays," Jacob said. "Maybe you could bring Philbert."

When they stopped by another pond to take a break and watch the ducks, Jacob said, "You really like Julia and those guys, don't you, Yvette?"

"Um—sort of," Holly told him. "I like Mary a lot, and Linda's okay most of the time. Julia—well, you kind of have to put up with her."

Jacob looked suddenly serious. "No, you don't. You don't at all. I don't think anyone has to put up with anyone who's mean. Julia's mean."

"I—I know. Mary says to just ignore her, so I do."

"Last year," Jacob said, "when Julia was still in sixth grade, someone in her class—your class now—told me that Julia got a kid in trouble by saying he cheated. She started this whole *thing* against him, so bad that a bunch of kids finally beat him up. Finally his family moved away."

"That's terrible!" Holly exclaimed. "Why did she do that?"

"She doesn't like anyone who's different from her, and that kid was black," Jacob said, shrugging. "Her family's like that, too, so I guess they've made her that way. Her mother made a big fuss last year, too, about a teacher someone thought was gay."

Holly felt cold inside again.

Jacob picked up his bike. "Anyway, you seem too nice to hang out with her." Quickly, as if that had embarrassed him, he hopped back on his bike and rode on. "It's a loop," he called over his shoulder. "If we go this way, we'll come out where we came in."

An Important Phone Call

Holly and Jacob went bike riding the next afternoon, and the next as well. Then it was Thursday and the Boywatchers mall day—the day before their meeting at Holly's house. Holly had been nervous about that all week. She knew Mom and KJ had gotten in a supply of Cokes and chips and pretzels, but she knew they'd want to say hello to the girls, too. What would she do if Mom and KJ touched each other, or if Julia noticed they wore matching rings on their left hands, or saw the gay magazine that they sometimes left out on the coffee table?

"It's time for Yvette to get her ears pierced," Julia said Thursday as soon as they were out of Julia's mother's car and walking through the entrance to the mall. "Come on, Yvette."

"But—" Holly protested. Of course she still wanted to,

but she hadn't asked Mom and KJ about it again, and she knew they'd be upset if she just went ahead and did it.

Julia linked her arm in Holly's and pulled her toward a small jewelry store with a sign in the window that proclaimed:

EAR PIERCING $15
PLUS FREE POST EARRINGS

"Oh, come on," Julia said. "Now that you're going out with nerdy faggy Jacob . . ."

Holly wrenched her arm out of Julia's and turned to face her. "I am not going out with him, and he's not nerdy or faggy!"

Julia shrugged. "Well, no," she said. "Bike riding's not really going out. I was just being kind. Yvette," she said with exaggerated patience, "look. Everyone has to start somewhere. And of course a faggy boy like Jacob . . ."

"He is *not* faggy!" Holly shouted, close to tears. And then, realizing that she'd just implied that being "faggy" was bad, she added, "And so what if he is?"

"Right," said Mary. "So what?"

Julia laughed. "If he is," she said with exaggerated patience, "there's no point in going out with him, is there? Unless you really are a fag hag. Maybe you're just scared of real boys. And maybe you're scared to have your ears pierced, too."

"N-no," Holly said nervously, sniffing. "I just have to ask Mom and KJ . . ."

She stopped, horrified.

"*Who?*" Julia asked. "Who's KJ, for heaven's sake?"

"Her *aunt*, Julia," Mary filled in quickly. "You met her at the mall, remember? Aunt Kate. Sometimes Yvette calls her KJ." She glanced anxiously at Holly. "Yvette told us she's a nurse, remember? So her opinion about ear piercing's, well, you know, valuable."

Julia laughed. "Oh, please," she said. "You'd think it was major surgery or something!"

"Julia . . ." Linda began, but Julia ignored her.

"Yvette," Julia said, "I'm just trying to help. You're kind of pretty, now that you're letting your hair grow. But you—well, you're kind of—tomboyish-looking, you know? Piercing your ears would help. Unless"—she regarded her closely, a little smirk playing around her lips—"unless of course you're going out with Jacob because you're, you know, like him. I guess some fag hags are really dykes."

"Oh, come on, Julia," Mary said. "Don't be ridiculous."

"You can't always tell," Julia said, "with girls."

"How do *you* know, Julia?" Mary said nastily—so nastily Holly was shocked; it didn't seem like Mary at all. "Maybe you're that way yourself, and you're just trying to hide it. Come on, Yvette." She tugged at Holly's sleeve. "Let's go look at the puppies."

Holly, still fighting tears, let Mary pull her away from Julia. Linda looked as if she wanted to follow them, but Julia grabbed her arm and led her off in the opposite direction.

"Here." Mary took a tissue out of her pocket and handed it to Holly. Gratefully, Holly wiped her eyes.

"Julia can be so mean," Mary said. "I don't think I want to

be her friend any more. Let's just you and me be friends, and never mind her and Linda. That boywatching stuff is embarrassing anyway. I think the boys think it's dumb. Babyish."

"I—I do, too." Holly stopped outside the pet store window. "But I've got to go ahead with having everyone over tomorrow. Julia'll be awful if I don't."

"You could make some excuse. You could, Yvette. You could say your mom's sick, or your aunt is, or something."

Holly shook her head. "No, I can't. Julia'd be worse if I did. Maybe afterward we could leave the Boywatchers Club, but not before."

Mary sighed. "I guess you're right." She looked into the window, where a tiny black-and-white puppy was gazing back at them, tail wagging, with one paw lifted. "Oh, wow," Mary said, "wouldn't you just die to have him? Come on, let's go in!"

That night, just as Holly was bracing herself to talk seriously to Mom and KJ about being careful the next afternoon around the Boywatchers, the phone rang. Will ran through the archway into the hall to answer it, and came sauntering back into the living room with an odd look on his face. He made a deep bow in front of Holly's chair, and in a fake English-butler voice announced, "Telephone call for Miss Yvette, if you please. A young gentleman, miss."

KJ and Mom looked up from their books, and Holly's stomach did a somersault. "Who?" she asked.

"I did not inquire, miss," Will said. "But if you like, I shall."

"No." Holly leapt up and ran to the phone. She stopped for a moment before she got there, and wiped her suddenly sweaty hands on her jeans. Then, very aware that everyone in her family was watching her, she picked up the phone, turned her back on all of them, and said softly, "Hello?"

"Yvette?" came a voice that sounded like Jacob's.

Holly swallowed hard, then cleared her throat. "Yes?"

"It—hi."

Silence.

"Um—hi?" Holly said. "Who—um—who is this?"

"Oh. Didn't I say?"

"No." Holly suppressed a giggle. Obviously, whoever it was—and she was pretty sure now that it was Jacob—was as nervous as she was.

"Oh. Well. It's Jacob."

Holly felt relieved enough to sit down. Then she felt nervous again. "Hi, Jacob," she managed to squeak.

"Hi. Did you—how was the mall?"

"Okay," Holly lied.

"Oh. Well, I was wondering, since Ralph and I went there and we saw Linda and Julia but we didn't see you and Mary. I was afraid you were—you know. Sick or something."

Holly felt herself smile. "No, I'm okay. You—um—you were nice to worry, though." Out of the corner of her eye she could see that Mom and KJ had turned back to their books, but it didn't look as if they were really reading. Will was watching her openly through the archway. But then KJ poked him and he started playing tug-the-string-bone with Philbert.

"Well," Jacob said, "well, I was—I was wondering if—if you could—um . . ." He laughed then. "Now I'm doing it."

"Doing what?"

"You know. Saying 'um.' I guess it's catching."

"Yeah, maybe." Holly didn't think that was as funny as Jacob, who was laughing nervously, seemed to, and she wished he'd finish asking what he'd started to ask. Was he going to ask her out? Really out, like for a date?

"Well, like I said, I—I was wondering if you'd like to—to go to the movies with me Saturday. It would have to be in the afternoon. I have to do something that night."

Holly's hands got sweaty again. He was! He really was asking her out! "Um—sure!" she said. She almost added "Thank you," but caught herself in time. "I'd love to," she said instead. "That would be neat. I guess I'll have to ask, though. Um—hang on, okay?"

"Okay." Jacob sounded relieved, and much more himself, even just with that one word.

Holly put the phone down carefully and went back into the living room.

"It's Jacob," she said to Mom and KJ. "You know. The boy I've been going bike riding with? He wants to know if I can go to the movies with him Saturday. Afternoon," she added quickly when Mom and KJ exchanged a glance. She ignored the violin-playing gestures Will was making with Philbert's string bone.

To Holly's relief, Mom and KJ both smiled. "Sure," they

both said at once, and then laughed. Mom got up and gave Holly a hug. "That's wonderful, honey," she said. "Just ask him which movie and which theater, could you, though?"

"And how you're getting there," KJ added. "Tell him we're old-fashioned—put it all on us if you're embarrassed."

Holly smiled back. "Okay," she said. "Um—thank you!" She spun around happily and almost danced back to the phone. "Jacob?"

"Yes?" He sounded as eager as she felt.

"It's okay," she said breathlessly. "Only . . ."

"Only what?" he interrupted quickly, anxiously.

"Only my—my mom wants to know what theater and what movie and how we're getting there."

"Yeah, my mom wanted to know that, too," he said. "How we're getting there anyway. There's only one theater. It's the Strand on Main Street—*The Trouble with Charley.* My sister says it's pretty good. There's a bike stand across the street, so we could ride. Or walk. It's really safe, tell your mom."

"Okay," Holly said. "Wait a minute. I'll go tell them—um—I'll tell her."

Trouble

Mom and KJ were fine when Holly told them what movie it was and about riding bikes to the Strand. "It's so exciting," KJ said, hugging her after she and Jacob had hung up. "A real date. Congratulations!"

"Oh, please!" Will looked disgusted.

"You just wait," Holly retorted, "till it's your turn."

"Not in your lifetime," Will said.

Mom laughed. "Don't be so sure, William Lawrence-Jones. Your turn's bound to come."

"Maybe not," Will said. "Maybe I'll be gay like you."

"Not likely," KJ answered promptly. "And even if you are, your turn's bound to come anyway. Holly?"

For Holly had looked away, remembering about the Boywatchers Club meeting, and about having to warn Mom and KJ—and Will, too—to be careful.

"Um," she said when everyone seemed ready to go back to their reading, "about tomorrow."

"Your club meeting," KJ said. "We've got Cokes and chips and . . ."

"Yes," said Holly. "I know. Thank you. It's something else."

"The new Holly?" Mom asked, frowning slightly. "I'll be at work till the usual time, but I'm sure KJ will remember to call you Yvette when she gets home. Will, you, too, if you're around."

"I'm going to Joey's," he said emphatically. "Believe me!"

"It's not just that." Holly hesitated. She wished there were some way to avoid saying the rest of it. Maybe they'd think of it themselves if she hinted, got them started. "It's also—well, you know." She paused, waiting.

KJ put her book down. "Know what?"

"Well . . ." Desperately, still not knowing how to say it, Holly picked up a copy of the gay news magazine Mom and KJ subscribed to. "It's just—well, for instance, would you mind if I put this away somewhere? And"—the words came out in a rush now. "And could you—one of you, anyway, in case everyone's still here when you get home, Mom—could one of you not wear your ring? And not—not—um—touch each other or anything, you know, like, call each other 'love' or anything? And Will, could you remember to call KJ Aunt Kate?"

Holly stopped. Mom, KJ, and Will were all staring at her as if she were a perfect stranger.

"Oh, wow," Will whispered finally. "You've really done it now, Holly!"

"Shh, Will," KJ said.

"Holly." Mom's voice shook a little. "We don't usually leave gay magazines and newspapers around when someone we don't know well is coming over. And we don't usually touch each other or call each other 'love' under those circumstances either."

"I know," Holly said miserably. "But I just wanted to make sure."

"You just wanted to make sure we all upheld your lie," Mom said angrily, her eyes probing Holly's. "What really upsets me is that you don't seem to trust us to be discreet."

"I—it's just that I know you don't want to hide," Holly said. "And—and Julia's pretty—pretty mean. She keeps calling Jacob faggy, and . . ."

"Is he?" KJ asked softly.

"No—I—I don't know," Holly moaned. "He's sweet and gentle and—and handsome, and he's not a jock, but I don't think he's faggy, and . . ."

"And you like him," Mom said, almost in her lawyer's voice now. "Right?"

"Right."

"And you go on seeing him—accepting him as he is—despite what Julia says."

"Yes."

"Well," Mom said, "shouldn't that apply to us, too?"

"It sure should," Will muttered.

"It—it does," Holly said. "It does, only—only . . ."

KJ got up and put her arms around Holly. "Only you're so caught up in being Yvette and in inventing a whole new family for yourself that you're scared to death there'll be a slip-up and then your new friends will know you have lesbian moms."

Holly nodded.

"Oh, Holly," KJ said. " 'What a tangled web we weave, when first we practice to deceive.' "

"Huh?" said Will. "Did I miss something? Holly's not a spider!"

"Sir Walter Scott," Mom said quietly. She looked at KJ, who nodded almost imperceptibly.

"All right," Mom said after a moment. "Once again, we'll go along with you as much as we can. But I don't think it's fair for us to have to take our rings off, or add to your lie. As it is, I'm very, very afraid that this whole thing is going to backfire on you someday. I wish you'd tell the truth, Holly."

"I can't," Holly whispered miserably. "I just can't."

Disaster

By Friday morning, when Holly left for school, there was no sign of any gay magazine or newspaper in the living room. Holly had hidden away her own small collection of gay books, books that she'd always kept in her room. Before breakfast, Mom came into the living room when Holly was checking the bookcase there for Mom and KJ's gay books. "They're in the guest room," Mom said stiffly. "I think everything's put away."

"Thank you," Holly said. Mom answered, "You're welcome," but she seemed tense all through breakfast, and Will yelled, "Come on, *Yvette*!" in an exaggerated voice when they were about to leave for school and work.

Holly thought she'd feel excited at school that day, and relaxed, since all the "evidence," as she'd come to call it, was gone. But, instead, she kept seeing Mom's tense face, and Will's disgusted one, and the pain she'd noticed in KJ's eyes when she'd kissed her goodbye at 6:30 that morning. Still, Julia acted friendly at lunch, and both Mary and Linda seemed excited about seeing where Holly lived.

"I can't wait to pat Philbert again," Mary said when they were finally on their way; Holly had left her bike at home and was walking with the others.

"He wouldn't be able to wait either, if he knew you were coming," Holly answered.

"Does he jump on people?" Linda asked, sounding anxious.

Holly grinned. "Only sometimes. Don't worry, I'll make him stay down. He'll be okay if someone who doesn't mind dogs goes in first."

"I'll go," Mary said promptly.

Julia said, "Thank goodness," but then she added, "What a pretty house!" when they turned down the front walk. She almost sounded as if she meant it, too.

"I think Julia's on her best behavior," Mary whispered when Holly opened the door. "At least so far."

Immediately Holly had to say, "Stay down, Philbert!" for Nutty Dog came bounding up, ears flapping and tail wagging. But right away Mary fell to her knees and hugged him, and he got calmer. Even Julia laughed when Mary said, "How do you do, Philbert?" and Philbert extended his paw.

"There's Cokes and stuff," Holly said. "We can get some and then go up to my room. Mom doesn't get home till six or so, but—um—Aunt Kate—will be here soon. She's on seven-to-three this week."

"That must be tough," said Linda, following Holly and the others into the kitchen. "To be on different shifts all the time. My father had to do that once . . ." Her voice trailed off.

"She tries to stay on seven-to-three as much as she can," Holly said quickly. "She usually has to stay for a while after three, telling the next shift about the patients. But she tries to be here around the time when my brother and I get home."

"That's really nice," Mary said. "Don't you think that's nice, Julia?"

"Mmmm." Julia was in front of the refrigerator, examining the decorations KJ had arranged so carefully on it soon after the Lawrence-Joneses had moved in. There were new layers in some places now, because each of them had kept finding old things they'd forgotten to add, and accumulating new ones.

"What's your mom's first name, Yvette?" Julia asked, peering under the cartoon with the Philbert-like dog on it.

"Lisa," Holly said without thinking—then froze in horror, for she saw that Julia had unearthed Mom's carefully preserved handmade valentine from last year. Obviously, all the Lawrence-Joneses had missed it when they'd been removing the "evidence."

"And like Mary said, KJ's your Aunt Kate, right?" She turned to Holly, an odd half-smile on her face. "Is she queer?"

Mary gasped and Linda said, "Julia!"

"Well, just look at this!" Julia held out the frilly valentine—a heart on a lace doily, with an arrow piercing the heart. "KJ + Lisa 4-ever" was printed on it in large red letters.

Holly tried to laugh. "Oh, that," she said in as offhand a voice as she could muster. "That's just a joke. I mean, they *are*—um—*sisters,* after all."

But Julia had turned the valentine over. "There's a fancy envelope stuck to the back of it, with hearts drawn all over it and 'For my love' written on it. That does seem kind of weird for sisters, don't you think, Linda?"

"I guess—I guess that envelope got there by mistake," Holly said quickly. "That one's—um—from—from KJ's—my aunt's—boyfriend. See, she has this boyfriend who lives really far away, and he . . ."

"Yeah, right," Julia said scornfully. "In India and he's going to send her a sari, like your dad. Besides, I thought your aunt was mourning her dead husband. Yvette," Julia said menacingly, "what's going on?"

Before Holly could answer, Mary stepped between them. "Shut up, Julia," she said. "Just shut up! It's none of our business."

"It's the club's business, Mary," Julia said. "Isn't it, Linda? I mean, it's the Boywatchers Club, after all. We can't have queers in it."

"If Yvette were queer," Linda said, "she wouldn't want to be in the club anyway. Come on, Julia, who cares about her aunt? Let's go up to your room, Yvette."

"Oh, let's," Julia said significantly. "I'd *love* to see the upstairs."

Holly's heart sank. Had Mom remembered to close the door to her room and KJ's? And the door to the study-guest room? There were four bedrooms upstairs, but it was pretty obvious that no one slept in the fourth one. And Mom and KJ's room had a queen-size bed in it.

"I—let me just make sure Will's decent," Holly said, pushing in front of the others. "You guys bring the Cokes and stuff. Coke's in the fridge, Mary—and the chips and pretzels are right there on the counter."

But Julia already had a bag of chips in her hand and she followed right behind Holly as Holly went upstairs. "I thought your brother was going to a friend's house," she said.

"Yeah, well, you never know with him." Holly reached the landing only a few steps ahead of Julia. Yes, the right doors were closed. Thank goodness!

"Why the closed doors?" Julia asked as Linda and Mary came up behind her. She put her hand on KJ and Mom's doorknob.

"Julia," Mary said, "that's none of your business."

"Messy rooms," Holly said lamely.

But Julia had already cracked the door open and peered in. "Whose room is this?" she asked.

"Um—Mom's," Holly said.

Julia grinned nastily. "She's got a nice big bed for when your dad comes home. *If* he comes home. And the room's not messy at all. That must be your brother's room," she went on, peering in through Will's open door, which revealed piles of clothes, comic books, and model plane parts. "So this one," she said, pausing outside the study-guest room after a quick glance into Holly's room—"must be your aunt's."

Before anyone could stop her, she'd opened the door and looked in.

And stared.

Holly closed her eyes, knowing what Julia and the others were seeing: A desk. Bookcases—with the gay books in and near them. An easy chair. A sofa. The sofa opened out into a bed, but you couldn't tell that from just looking at it.

"Your aunt sure doesn't have much of a bedroom." Julia frowned. "This doesn't look like a bedroom at all."

Holly suddenly felt very tired, and incapable of lying any more.

But I have to lie, she thought. I can't stop now. I can't!

"She—she's studying for—for a supervisor's job," she said weakly, reaching around Julia for the door and pulling it closed. "So she needs the desk. And she's very neat. She's got a big closet, too, a walk-in one with—with drawers. And the sofa really opens into . . ."

"I don't believe you." Julia smiled coldly. "I think there's a mystery going on here, Holly-Yvette Lawrence-Jones, and I think the Boywatchers Club has a right to know what it is. Right? Right, Linda? Linda!"

"Right," Linda answered, but not very firmly.

"No," Mary said. "You didn't snoop around in my house, Julia, or Linda's either. So why should you snoop in Yvette's?"

"You and Linda and I have known each other since third grade," Julia said. "And we've always been in each other's houses."

"Yes, but not in our parents' rooms or anything."

"I don't remember closed doors in your house, Mary, or

in Linda's, either. No, this is a house with secrets in it." Julia looked straight at Holly, as if she were trying to look through her. "Weird secrets. And I think I know what they are, too.

"I don't think that woman you call your aunt is your aunt at all," Julia went on, while Mary and Linda stared at her openmouthed and Holly tried not to cry. "I think she's your mother's lover. I think your mother's a dyke, Yvette. No wonder you like faggy Jacob. For all we know, you're a dyke, too."

"Julia, shut up," Mary said in a low, insistent voice. "Just shut up!" She put a protective arm around Holly's shoulder.

"I wouldn't touch her if I were you, Mary," Julia said. "She might touch you back or grab you or something. Anyway, we certainly don't want any dykes in the Boywatchers Club." Julia spun around and started down the stairs. "Are you coming?" she called over her shoulder. "Come on, Linda, Mary!"

Linda hesitated, but then, with an apologetic glance at Holly, she followed Julia. Mary stayed put, but then went to the head of the stairs.

"Yvette and I don't want to be in the Boywatchers Club anyway," Mary called at Julia's retreating back. "It's dumb and babyish and the boys think it's dumb, too."

"See if we care," Julia called back from the foot of the stairs. "You're probably just as queer as Yvette."

Holly heard the front door click and then KJ's voice saying, "Hi, girls. Is the meeting over already?"

Holly burst into tears.

KJ Guesses

Several things happened very quickly: Philbert barked, and KJ's voice, which had sounded so cheerful at first, suddenly changed to sounding concerned as she said, "What on earth's the matter?" Then, obviously really worried, she called, "Holly?" At the same time, Mary tightened her arm around Holly, saying, "Shh, Yvette, shh, mean old Julia's not worth crying about, and Linda's just too weak to stand up for herself." And then, to make matters worse, as Holly heard KJ's footsteps on the stairs, she also heard Will come bursting through the front door, shouting, "Hey, everyone, we won, we won! Joey had to go someplace with his mom, but he and I raced this big kid, and . . ."

Then for a moment everyone was silent, even Philbert, even Will, while they all ran upstairs to her and to Mary, who stepped back as soon as KJ reached her. "It's just those awful girls," Mary said to KJ. "They've been calling Yvette names."

Holly buried her face against KJ, still sobbing.

"What names?" KJ asked, holding Holly, gently rubbing her back.

Holly wrenched herself away from KJ. "Just dumb names. It's all right, I'm all right now." She rubbed her eyes, wiped her nose with the back of her hand, and tried to smile. "K—Aunt Kate—calls me Holly, still, at home," she tried to explain to Mary. "Not—not just when she's mad like we—like I said at the mall. You know, my official name instead of my nickname."

Mary was staring at her, sympathy mingled with what looked like fear or worry or even shock on her face. "It's all right, Yvette," she said softly. "I don't care what your name is. And I don't believe anything Julia said. Like I said, she's always been that way—mean to people, especially new people." Mary touched Holly's shoulder tentatively. "It's okay. I—I'd better go. I'll call you later. Or you can call me. Goodbye, Mrs.—um—Ms. Lawrence-Jones."

KJ, her eyes still on Holly, said, "Goodbye, Mary. Thank you. Will, could you see—Yvette's guest out?"

"Sure, but . . ."

"Will!"

"Okay, okay."

And then Holly and KJ were alone at the top of the stairs, except for Philbert, who, whimpering, kept nosing Holly as if he wanted to comfort her, too. Gently, with Philbert following, KJ led Holly into her room and sat both herself and Holly down on the edge of Holly's bed. "Now," she said, "I think you'd better tell me what happened and why those other two girls were running out of the house as I was coming in."

Holly shook her head fiercely, and threw herself down, burying her face against the pillow.

"Holly, please!" KJ rubbed Holly's back again, the way she and Mom had done when Holly was little and had had a bad dream. "I can't help if I don't know."

But Holly knew she couldn't speak, couldn't say anything to KJ, or Mom, or Will, or anyone. And Kelsey was too far away.

Kelsey, she thought fiercely, blocking out KJ's soothing voice, making herself deaf to her soft words. It's Kelsey's fault. It was her idea. The Plan had been her idea. Hadn't it? Sure, it had. Anyway, Kelsey'd encouraged her, egged her on . . .

Anger filled her, and she clenched her fists, sobbing again, beating her fists on the pillow . . .

But KJ seized them, held them, said sharply, "Holly! Holly, stop it!"

In a softer voice, KJ continued. "I'm guessing that your lie did backfire, Holly, just as Mom feared it would. I'm guessing that those girls found out you'd been lying to them, and that they said something cruel. There's no excuse for cruelty, but remember this: People don't like being lied to. They don't like finding out that something they believed to be true isn't true." KJ bent and kissed the back of Holly's head. "I wish my loving, honest, friendly, happy Holly would come back. I like her much better than I like Yvette, sweetie. So does Mom and so does Will. Nutty Dog, too, I bet." KJ stood and Holly felt her patting the bed as if inviting Philbert to jump up on it. Ordinarily, he wasn't allowed on any of their beds, but KJ went on patting until Holly felt him jump up and curl himself next to her. Then she heard KJ leave the room, and she put her arms around Philbert and sobbed bitterly into his soft hair.

A Decision?

It was dark outside when Holly opened her eyes again. Her pillow was wet with tears. Nutty Dog, still beside her, thumped his tail against her leg and looked so expectantly into her face, the way he did when he wanted to be taken for a walk or to play ball, that for a moment she laughed, forgetting why he was there and what had happened.

Then it all came crashing back: Julia finding the valentine, opening closed doors, saying awful words—accusing her, Holly, of being gay; calling KJ a dyke, a queer . . .

Stiffly, Holly sat up and looked around her room. I never really did want that dressing table, she thought, and I never got my ears pierced. My hair's getting long, but it's even harder to comb. I still have a big behind and sometimes I forget Yvette's handwriting. Maybe I really never did become Yvette.

She remembered what Mary had said about leaving the Boywatchers Club.

But then she remembered what Linda had said, too—that if she, Holly, were gay, she wouldn't want to be in the Boywatchers Club in the first place.

So how could she leave? Maybe Mary could, but she couldn't.

Could she?

What if she *were* gay?

There must be worse things to be, she thought, since Mom and KJ are gay, and they're really super people.

"But I don't want to be gay," Holly whispered. "I don't!"

She remembered that KJ had said she doubted that Will would be gay, when he'd joked about it. And she remembered how much she herself wanted to be with Jacob, and that she had a date with him. And that one of her books—one of the books she'd hidden in the study-guest room—said that children of gay parents are no more likely to grow up gay than are children of straight parents.

So maybe she wouldn't have to worry about that. And maybe she *could* leave the Boywatchers Club.

I really do like Jacob, she thought. And I bet he's not gay, no matter what Julia calls him. Julia calls everyone names. Even Jacob said so. Julia's just plain mean.

Like those kids at camp last summer. They were mean, too, like Julia. Picking on anyone who's different.

Holly gave Philbert a hug. She got up and opened her

bottom desk drawer, where she kept her diaries. She took out the new one—she hadn't written in it for a long time—and put it on top of her desk. But then she pulled out her old ones, sat down, and began thumbing through them, reading here and there. She wasn't sure what she was looking for at first, reading random entries:

Dear Diary,

Hello. Happy birthday to me. I'm 9 today. Mom and KJ let me have a big party and 15 kids came! We went to the zoo and then we came back and had ice cream. Kelsey stayed over and we stayed up till 10 watching a tape of *Bambi.* It was awesome! Nutty Dog ate almost all the popcorn, and we wrestled with him on the floor . . .

Dear Diary,

Georgie Brisk sent me a valentine! He's nicer than the other boys. He's cute, too . . .

Dear Diary,

Aunt Yvette took me and Will to the ice show. The best part was a sort of a play, with people dressed up as animals. I wish I could ice skate. I think I'd like racing, though, not the fancy stuff. You know, racing like in the Olympics . . .

Dear Diary,

Mom had to have something called a root canal. She and KJ were up all last night because her tooth hurt so bad. Will and I made supper for everyone tonight. We made soup for Mom because she still feels horrible. KJ is worried about her and so are we. But KJ says she'll be okay . . .

Dear Diary,

Mom's tooth is much better! Hooray! We all took Nutty Dog to the park and played Frisbee. On the way back, Will made us all hold hands and then he said, "I like us. I really like us!" He made us say that "All for one and one for all" thing, too.

Will can be weird, but he's right. I like us, too . . .

Tears filled Holly's eyes suddenly. "I like us," she whispered. "I still like us."

Yvette isn't part of that, she thought. Yvette probably wouldn't play Frisbee with Nutty Dog, or hold hands with her whole family, or make soup, or go to the zoo, or like people pretending to be skating animals, or want to race on ice skates.

Yvette probably wouldn't even ride a bike.

She certainly wouldn't play soccer.

Holly closed her old diaries and picked up the new one. A piece of paper—no, a card—fluttered out, the card Mom and KJ and Will and Philbert had given her for her birthday.

She opened it and read the poem again:

The holly and the ivy,
When they are both full grown,
Of all the trees that are in the wood,
The holly wears the crown.

Softly, she touched her hair. It was longer now, with waves cascading nearly to her shoulders, just as she'd thought she wanted.

Unruly waves, though, hard to comb.

Yvette was the one who wanted waves, she thought.

Holly liked short hair.

Likes short hair.

She reached for the scissors.

The New Plan

Saturday morning was bright and sunny, a crisp fall day, perfect for a bike ride. Maybe not so perfect for being indoors at the movies, but that was going to be special, too, in a different way. Besides, there was still the morning.

And there was a lot to do.

The night before, when Holly had shown Mom and KJ and Will her new short haircut, and explained to them what had really happened with Julia and Linda, they'd all talked until they'd made a new Plan—the Plan Holly was about to put into effect. And then they'd hugged, and KJ made Holly a paper crown, which was supposed to be like the one in the poem. She put it on Holly's head, saying, "Welcome back, Holly," and Nutty Dog barked and leapt around them like crazy.

Later, Holly wrote Kelsey a long letter telling her how The Plan had backfired. "It did sound like a good idea, Kelse," she wrote at the end, "but I think I like Holly better than Yvette. I didn't know The Plan was going to hurt everyone so much. And it was too hard being someone else all the time. I hope you understand!"

She wasn't mad at Kelsey anymore, and she realized it had been herself she'd been mad at, too. After all, they'd figured out The Plan together. And she was pretty sure Kelsey would understand about giving it up. Kelsey always understood.

But now there was Mary to explain to, and that was going to be harder. Holly's stomach felt queasy as she biked to Mary's house after calling and inviting herself over. Her stomach cramped when she saw Mary waiting outside.

"Hi, what's up?" Mary called from her front steps. "Are you okay? Hey, I like your hair! It's really cute."

"Thank you," Holly answered, jumping off her bike and trying to ignore her stomach. "And yes, I'm fine. Um—thank you for yesterday."

"That's okay. So are we going to leave the Boywatchers Club?"

"I'd like to," Holly said. "Only—just if you still want to. I . . ."

"Of course I still want to!"

"No, I mean—Mary, I've got to tell you something. I—my name isn't really Yvette at all. It's really Holly. Yvette's not even a nickname or anything. I just decided I wanted to be someone else. Someone named Yvette, after my aunt."

Mary smiled. "That's okay," she said. "I kind of guessed.

There were things you said that made me wonder. I did the same thing once, too, pretended to be someone else, only I was really little and I couldn't keep it up. I think you were pretty good at it, but it's hard, isn't it?"

Holly closed her eyes for a moment in relief. "We didn't have a doorman in New York," she said. "Or take taxis, at least not very often." Then she opened her eyes and took a deep breath. "That's not all," she said. "Um—Julia was right."

Mary tipped her head inquisitively. "Julia, *right*?" she said with a laugh. "Oh, no! I like it much better when she's wrong!"

"Julia was right about my mom and KJ," Holly said, carefully watching for Mary's reaction. "You know, the person I've been calling Aunt Kate. She's not my aunt, she's—um—my other mom. Will and I are adopted. And—um—Mom and KJ are gay. They love each other. You know. Really love each other, like—um—like they were married, or—well, like that."

Mary stared at her for a long minute. Holly stared back, hardly daring to breathe. Then Mary said, very softly, "It doesn't matter. Are you gay, too?"

Holly's stomach cramped again. "I don't think so."

Slowly, Mary nodded. "That wouldn't have mattered either. But I'd want to know. No wonder you wanted to be someone else. Julia would never understand about having two moms. It must be tough, though. Is it?"

"Sometimes," Holly admitted, and then realized how relieved she was to be able to say that.

"Were they mad at you for pretending?"

"Hurt more than mad. And that was awful. I—I love them a lot."

Mary sat down on her front step. "Well," she said, "I like KJ. And I like your other mom, too, even though I only saw her that once, on the mountain. So what if they're gay? My parents have a gay friend," she went on. "A guy. He's really nice. He comes for dinner sometimes." She paused for a moment. "I'm glad we're leaving the Boywatchers Club. Julia and Linda could get pretty rotten if they found out about your moms. Julia, anyway."

"I'm going to tell them," Holly said firmly. "I know Julia will be mean. But Mom and KJ said it'd probably be worse if Julia spreads rumors than if she's mean because of the truth."

"Yeah," said Mary. "Yeah, I bet they're right. But what about Jacob?"

Holly took another deep breath. "I'm going to tell him, too. I think he'll be okay about it. And if he isn't, then I don't want to go out with him any more."

"Holly Lawrence-Jones," said Mary, putting her arm over Holly's shoulder. "You are one brave person." She grinned. "That old Yvette," she said, "I guess she was kind of a coward. But my best friend Holly's really brave."

Soccer, Anyone?

Holly was so tense at the movie that she almost didn't feel it when Jacob took her hand, and when she realized he had, she felt even tenser. It was a different kind of tension, though, excited instead of scared. Jacob's hand felt sweaty, and she knew hers must also, and she sat there quietly, hardly daring to move. *A boy is holding my hand*, she kept thinking. *A boy who thinks my name is Yvette, and who I'm going to have to tell the truth to . . .*

Then, suddenly, just as the movie ended and the credits started rolling, Jacob leaned over closer to her, still holding her hand, and gave her a quick kiss on the cheek.

Holly was so surprised she heard herself give a little squeak, and Jacob laughed.

Then the house lights came on, and Holly saw that he was blushing.

"You're blushing," he said to her as they got up.

"So're you!"

"I guess maybe we're not very good at this yet," he said. He held up their two hands, then gave hers a squeeze and let go.

Holly surreptitiously dried her hand on her jeans. "I guess not," she said, wishing her heart would stop beating so hard. She started to go out into the aisle.

But Jacob put his hand out and stopped her. "Is it okay?" he asked.

"Um—what? Is what okay?"

"There you go again with the ums," he said, grinning. "Is it okay that we—you know. Are friends. Go out, I guess, sometimes, even. You know. Not just bike rides."

"I—sure," Holly said. "Only . . ."

His face fell. "Only what?"

"Only," she said firmly, hating it, forcing herself, "only I've got to tell you something first. Something that might change your mind."

He looked relieved. "Nothing's going to change my mind. But okay. Sure. You want to get a Coke or a burger or something?"

"Okay."

Out in the bright afternoon sunlight, Holly wished she hadn't said anything, wished she'd just let him go on believing whatever he believed about her. But she knew that wouldn't work at school, once she'd told Julia and the others. And if The New Plan was going to work as she and

Mom and KJ and Will—and she and Mary—had discussed, it would be awful if she hadn't told Jacob in advance.

Still, a few minutes later, seated opposite Jacob behind a big glass of Coke, she wasn't sure she'd be able to do it. Suddenly it was much, much harder than she'd imagined. Maybe he'd be disgusted, or angry. Maybe he'd laugh. Maybe he wouldn't want to see her anymore. She found herself wrestling with all the worries Mom and KJ had told her and Will that they felt themselves each time they needed to tell someone they were lesbians.

At least, she thought gratefully, I don't have to say that. At least it's not me who's gay.

But that won't make any difference to Julia, she told herself. And maybe it won't to Jacob, either.

"So," Jacob said, smiling at her disarmingly. "What's this big thing you have to tell me that I'm going to hate?"

"My name's not Yvette," she began. "It's Holly." Then, trying not to look hard enough at Jacob to be stopped by his reaction, if he reacted, which he didn't seem to be doing, she told him about her parents, the words pouring out so quickly they sometimes stumbled into one another. "They love each other," she finished. "Mom and KJ. They love me and Will, too."

She had to stop there for breath.

"Do you love them?" Jacob looked more curious than shocked.

"Yes," Holly said, gulping. She felt as if she was about to hiccup like a little kid who's been crying. Only of course she hadn't been—well, maybe inside, some. "Oh, yes!"

Jacob shrugged. "So what's the big deal?" he said. "Lots of

kids don't love their parents, and lots more don't admit that they do. If you do, and you can say it to people, you're lucky. Who cares if your parents are both women?"

"Lots of people," Holly said weakly.

Jacob shook his head. "No. Not lots of people. A few. Julia. Maybe Linda. Linda follows Julia around like she's her dog or something. And I told you about Julia. Nothing anyone can say will make Julia a human being. So who cares about her? She doesn't count." Jacob reached across the table and took Holly's hand. "Now, how about what I asked? Is it okay if we go out together? I have to tell you something, too. I never had a girlfriend before . . ."

On Monday morning, Julia didn't speak to Holly, even though Holly tried to speak to her. And she pulled Linda past Holly as if Holly didn't exist.

"I'm going to tell them now," Holly said to Mary as they went into the lunchroom at noontime. She'd already asked her teachers to call her Holly, and told the school secretary to cross out Yvette on her records.

Mary, though she looked pale, nodded and said, "I'll come with you."

"You don't have to."

"I want to. Let's go."

So both of them walked briskly over to the Boywatchers Club table, and Holly tried not to notice when Julia turned away as if Holly wasn't there. Linda toyed with her sandwich, looking embarrassed.

"I've got something to tell you," Holly said.

"Did you hear a voice?" Julia asked Linda. When Linda didn't answer, Julia poked her and asked again.

"N-no," Linda stammered, still toying with her sandwich.

"That's what I thought," said Julia. "Did you do the math?"

"Julia," said Holly, "I'm going to tell you something whether or not you want to listen. You were right about my moms. And Yvette isn't my nickname. Holly's my only name. I tried to be someone else because I didn't want anyone to know my moms are gay. But that was dumb."

"So you're a liar, too," Julia said nastily.

Linda looked up and stared, first at Julia and then at Holly.

Holly hesitated, surprised. She'd imagined a lot of reactions from Julia, but not that one.

"Yes, I guess I am a liar," Holly said. "At least I was one. But I'm not one any more."

"She lied because of mean people like you, Julia," Mary said. "Like I told you, we don't want to be in your stupid club any more. We don't want to be with mean, bossy people, and . . ."

"Neither do I," Linda burst out, suddenly pushing her chair back and standing up. Holly was startled to see tears in Linda's eyes. "I'm sorry, Holly. We really were mean. I don't care about your moms. At least you've got two parents. I wish I did."

Holly felt herself begin to smile.

"Come on, Holly, Linda," said Mary, tugging them both

away. "I'm starving. And we've got to go see if we can talk the coach into letting us sign up for indoor soccer this winter. I don't think it's too late for that."

The three of them walked away from Julia, arm in arm, with Holly in the middle.

Julia glowered at them, and then went over to another table and started whispering to the girls there. The girls looked up and stared at Holly, and a couple of them giggled.

But from across the lunchroom, Jacob clasped his hands together over his head and, grinning, waved them at Holly.